To everyone who likes their romance stories a little dysfunctional.

DYSFUNCTIONAL

WARNINGS

This is a dark romance, and while everyone's levels of dark may vary, there might be disturbing content in here for some of you. Dysfunctional is intended for mature audiences due to the graphic nature of both violence and sexual acts. Find more detailed warnings on my website. www. isabellucero.com

EZRA

EZRA.

CHAPTER
ONE

He doesn't think anybody's watching because he's used to being the stalker. He's too cocky. Too sure that nobody will notice what he's doing. I see him, though.

In the corner booth of The Perfect Blend—a local coffee house in Soledad Square, Vermont, I peer over my newspaper and watch as the man smiles charmingly at the waitress as she delivers his order. It's a plain black coffee because he thinks anything else would be too memorable. However, almost nobody orders plain coffee, so he stands out more than he thinks he does.

When a woman sits at a table across from him, I know that it's her he has his eye on. She's blonde, attractive in an average way, and young enough to be naive.

He's pretty good, not doing too much to be obvious. He doesn't look up from his sketchbook for almost three minutes, focusing on whatever he's drawing while sporadically running a finger under his bottom lip. When he does look up, his eyes land on her, move to his book, then he does a double-take. The girl's eyes were already on him, so

1

she gives him a shy grin when he locks onto her the second time.

His lips turn up on one side as he runs a hand through his hair in a boyish way before going back to drawing. He plays this game well. Show enough interest, pretend to not be a predator, and get your prey to come to you.

Once the girl's coffee is delivered, she takes a few sips, her eyes constantly dancing toward the handsome man in front of her. With half the drink down, she finally gets up and makes her way to his table.

I should warn her—get up and intervene. Instead, I settle in and watch how this plays out.

She creeps over, like she doesn't want to startle him, but he knows she's coming. He anticipated it. He jolts, though, pretending to be scared, and then they share a laugh before he offers her the free chair at his table. She gestures to his sketchbook, and he hesitantly displays it to her. Her hands go to her lips, her mouth ajar, shocked at his apparent talent. The man closes the book and hugs it to his chest, playing modest and shy. They talk for another thirty minutes before he gets up, glancing at the watch clasped around his tattooed wrist. She watches him, expectantly, waiting for him to ask for her number, maybe a date. He puts money on the counter and leaves, the bell ringing above the door. She looks disappointed until thirty seconds later when he appears right outside the storefront window, scratching his tilted head as he gazes back at her with a crooked smile.

She gets up and meets him outside, and once again they share a laugh before he jerks his thumb over his shoulder. She nods, her grin wide, and they take off together.

I shake my head, sighing as I put down the paper. The

waitress left my check several minutes ago, so I leave a ten on the table and get up to follow them.

Unaware, like every other person in this quiet, *safe* town, they amble down the cobblestone road, oblivious to the killer among them. In this case, there's two. Now, I don't have proof of what this man does with these women, but considering I never see them reemerge after he's set his eyes on them, I can only assume he does away with them in a permanent fashion.

It's not like I have much room for judgment. My moral compass is broken beyond repair, but this man seems to solely focus on women, and I can't help but wonder why. Color me intrigued. I have to know more, because I've never met another person like me.

I first caught wind of this guy a couple months back when I noticed him spending time with a woman who worked at the convenience store I frequent to grab my cigarettes. She'd take her breaks to eat with him in the small food court area, then one day, weeks later, she no longer worked there. After that, I started paying closer attention.

The second woman was someone who went to the community college. He conveniently ran into her in a library, like this crazy motherfucker reads books. Not to say that just because he's covered in tattoos, has a piercing through his nose, and occasionally has black painted nails means he's not capable of reading. But unless it's a *how-to* on stalking, I don't see this guy spending much time with his nose in a book.

I saw him by chance, through a window as I was working outside, and then I kept coming back. He was there pretending to be consumed by *The Handmaid's Tale* when she noticed him. I expect it was the book that kept her away. She probably thought he was reading it for tips and ideas on how to abuse women. Not the best choice. So the next time we were all there, he was reading *A Vindication of the Rights of Woman*, which made my eyes roll to the back of my head. Trying too hard. But it worked. She finally approached him when he took a break to take a sip of his coffee.

They met up a few more times, until they didn't. I tried following them on that last evening, not knowing it would be the final one, but of course, I got pulled away by a phone call from work.

I've made a few more visits to the library, wondering if she'd show back up, but she hasn't. Just like the convenience store girl. Neither have been reported missing, but I still feel the need to keep a close eye on him.

With a soft touch on the small of her back, he directs her into a red brick building. I hang back so as to not be too obvious. Scrutinizing the three-story structure that curves around the corner, I wonder why he'd bring a victim to a somewhat busy hotel.

Thirty seconds after they disappear inside, I enter, my eyes roaming the lobby for their figures. I worry briefly when I don't spot them right away, but I recognize the plaid button up stretching across his back as they enter a hallway.

With quick, yet calm steps, I head in their direction. Someone touches my arm, attempting to ask me a question, but I hardly hear what she says and offer a polite, if not tight smile. "I'm sorry. I'm late for a meeting."

If she's offended, I don't stick around long enough to see the hurt on her face. I dart around the corner and watch the blue and black plaid shirt vanish through a doorway to the right.

Is he killing them in a hotel? How would he get them out?

When I come across the archway he went under, I realize it's not a door to a room as I assumed. I push open the door to the bathroom, curious as to what I may see when I step inside, but I don't get far.

He shoves me against the white subway tiles that cover the wall, his forearm pressing into my throat.

"Why the fuck are you following me?"

TWO

I push him off of me. "I'm not following you!"

"Right. You always trail people from coffee houses to hotels?" he asks, stepping into my space again.

Shit. He's more aware than I thought. When I don't come up with a response quick enough, his lips draw up into a wicked snarl.

"I thought so. So, what the fuck do you want from me, huh?"

No use in pretending. I've been curious about this guy for months, so I might as well jump right in and see what happens.

"I want to know what you were doing with that woman."

His brows furrow briefly, his head cocking to the side. "What woman?"

I straighten my back, feeling smug as I get the upper hand. "You just said I followed you from the coffee house to this hotel. What makes you think I only saw you?" He stares back at me. "Or do you mean *which* woman?" I arch a brow, waiting for a reply.

The briefest flash of concern crosses his eyes before he smothers it, loosening his shoulders as he slips his hands into the pockets of his jeans. "She your girl or something?"

"I don't have a girl."

"You want her?" he questions, pointing as if she's standing next to us.

"No. That's not why I'm asking."

He rolls his eyes and goes to the sink, giving me his back like I can't see his reflection in the mirror. It's a pretty classic move to keep someone from seeing the fear in your eyes or the lies on your lips. He's putting on an act because that's what he does. But I've been doing that for years. I can see the signs.

"I don't know what the hell you're talking about, man. I brought a girl here to fuck. If she's not yours then I don't see the issue." He finishes washing his hands before heading to the paper towel dispenser. "I think you're just a fucking weirdo stalker."

"*I'm* the stalker?"

He spins around. "Who else?"

I want to yell, *you, motherfucker!* But I don't. "Is she waiting in the room for you now?"

"Do you want to join us? Is that what this is about? Kinda weird to fixate on a random couple, but I'm not opposed to threesomes."

This fucking guy. He's making me sound like him. *Stalker. Fixate.* Well, I guess he's not too off the mark, but he doesn't need to know that.

I call his bluff, simply because I want to see if this girl is really waiting for him in a room or if he ditched her when he realized I was on his tail, therefore unable to go through with what he really wanted to do.

"Yeah. I'll join you."

7

His eyes widen and he chokes out a laugh. "You're fucking crazy, man. You know that, right?" He pushes past me and into the hall. I follow.

"You offered."

"It's like when someone says, *call me if you ever need anything.* It's something you say when you don't actually expect them to take you up on it."

Which is what I figured and why I said yes.

"So, you're taking your offer back?" I ask, trailing him as he struts down the hall.

He laughs again, shaking his head. "No. You can come." The last word drips with innuendo as he emphasizes it, angling his head over his shoulder.

We turn a corner and he digs into his pocket for the key. I begin to worry that maybe I misjudged the situation. Just because he's a stalker and potentially a killer of women doesn't mean he can't rent a hotel room to fuck someone in. Everyone needs to get laid. However, I'm not so sure I want to be involved in this. Maybe he's calling my bluff, and now I don't know how to get out of it.

He seems to know what I'm thinking as he throws me a glance before opening the door, a smug little grin on his face.

I follow him inside, my eyes scanning the room. There's no girl in sight. He heads toward the bathroom, disappearing for a few seconds before reemerging with a shrug. "I guess she left."

My eyes stay focused on him, narrowing slightly as I search for any tells. He holds my gaze, face stoic.

"That's too bad," I say.

"Yes. Yes, it is."

I take a step backward. "I guess I'll go then."

He takes a step forward. "Sure." His grin is forced and tight.

I continue to move toward the door without turning my back on him. I'm not stupid. I reach for the knob and turn. His eyes burn with unfurled frustration and his jaw remains tense as he watches me. He's pissed I ruined his plans, and I don't think it's just that I was a cock block. He had a devious agenda, and I've thwarted it, ruining what was probably weeks of planning. Do I feel bad? Not really. But I understand.

"See you around."

His smile turns wicked. "I'm sure you will."

SOLEDAD SQUARE IS one of the smallest towns in Vermont. It's almost hard to avoid people. You'd think someone like me would go to a bigger and busier place—somewhere like New York City or LA, but I also hate people. I'd kill more of them if they were constantly running into me, so self-involved they've lost all sense of politeness.

They say kindness goes a long way, and it's true. Plenty of people have probably had their lives spared simply for being kind to a person who would later snap and massacre everyone who did them wrong. I can say with confidence that everyone who ever crossed me got what was coming to them, and I don't regret it. Well, maybe that's not true. Most deserved it. Some were victims of circumstance, but it's not like I target preschool teachers or anything. However, I've been trying to rehabilitate myself. Something I was sure wasn't possible, but it's been nearly two years and nobody's died by my hand in that time.

However, the cage holding my monster captive is rattling.

Since this place is so small, though, I see *him* quite often, and since our altercation at the hotel, he lets it be known he's aware I'm there, too. I'm not even trying to track him. We just end up in the same spots sometimes. I haven't noticed him talking to any new women, but I think it's because he's afraid I'm onto him.

A week after our encounter in the hotel, I'm back in The Perfect Blend, having a coffee and watching the news on the TV they have hoisted up in a corner. Even though it's been a long time since I've killed anyone, I still wait for the day I'm found out. I wonder if my picture will ever pop up on the screen with the word *wanted* underneath. My last kill was a little more high-profile than I wanted. It's why I've tried controlling myself.

My waitress, Janeen, appears next to me with a friendly smile. "Do you need anything else?"

I shake my head. "No. I'm good. Thank you."

She nods and heads back behind the counter, waving at someone who walks through the door. My eyes move to the recipient of her wave, and surprise blankets my face. It's the woman who walked to the hotel with the stalker. She's alive.

I scratch at my jaw before turning my attention to my phone. A few minutes into reading a news article, someone slides into the seat across from me. I lift my head and come face-to-face with him. I know he goes by Kas because I asked about him already.

He smiles, scooting to the end where he can lean his back against the wall and have a view of the room. "She's back," he says with a quick gesture.

"Yeah. I see that."

"You looked a little surprised to see her walk in."

"Did I?" I muse, dropping my eyes to my phone.

He was watching me and I didn't even know he was here.

"Why would you be surprised?" he asks, voice jovial, though I know it's an act.

"I wasn't."

He laughs. "Okay."

He's quiet for a while, and I finally start getting annoyed. "Do you need something from me?" I ask, putting my phone down a little too hard when I look at him.

His eyes roam my face, a small smile on his lips as his gaze lowers before meeting my eyes again. "I don't know. Maybe."

When he doesn't elaborate, I huff. "Are you gonna say anything else?"

"Why are you so tense, man?" He laughs. "I just wanted to know if you wanted to hang out sometime? Maybe go to a bar and get a drink."

My brows furrow. "Why would I want to do that?"

"Why not?" he counters, not offended in the least. "Every time I see you, you aren't with anyone. You don't seem to have friends."

"Every time you see me?" I repeat back to him.

He shrugs. "It's a small town."

I eye him carefully before I respond. "Do *you* have friends?"

He laughs again, but the thing about his laughter is, it never feels genuine. "No, man. I guess I don't. That's why I'm asking you. I'm still kinda new here."

"How new?"

"Less than a year."

"Well, I'm not from here, so if you're looking for a tour guide or information expert, it's not me."

"Oh yeah?" he questions, cocking his head. "Where did you come from?"

I don't want to answer. He seems too curious. With a sigh, I say, "Sure. I'll go out with you. When and where?"

His lips stretch into a smile that would send chills down the back of anybody except me. It's like he knew I wouldn't want to answer.

THREE

I show up to The Hideaway—the pub he chose to meet up at—and find it buzzing with a variety of clientele. Men in their fifties and sixties line the bar, women in their twenties screech with excitement when one of their friends brings them another round of shots, and guys in their late thirties or early forties drink beer, their eyes bouncing from the women to the TV in the corner.

After sidling up to the end of the bar, the bartender approaches and I order a beer.

"Beer?" a voice says from behind me. "Get something stronger. Tequila or whiskey."

It's him, a forced grin on his lips as he nods to the man behind the bar.

The bartender turns his eyes back to me. "I'll stick with the beer."

"Let me get a Gin and Tonic," he says, shifting to the side to face me. "So, you made it. To be honest, I didn't think you'd show."

"I figured I'd see you again and you'd just keep bothering me."

He snorts. "Sure. You can just admit to wanting to come."

Once we pay for our drinks, we turn and simultaneously make our way to the corner booth that gives us a view of almost the entire bar.

I take a swig as I catalog the room.

"Looking for a victim?"

With a furrowed brow, I angle my head over my shoulder and survey him. "What are you talking about?"

He laughs, his body relaxed before he brings the glass to his lips. "A woman. Someone to take home tonight."

My eyes find the two tables full of women. "Nah."

"None of them are your type?" he questions.

"Not really."

"There's blondes, brunettes, redheads, tall, short, plump, and skinny girls. How is none of that your type?"

I take another gulp. How do you explain that nobody's your type because most people are normal? "I don't really do relationships. They haven't worked out well for me in the past."

"So, your type is temporary."

"Exactly."

"I can understand that."

I bet you can.

I sit back and scoot over since he's too close to my left and I want to be able to see him fully. I figure now's as good a time as ever to ask him the same type of questions.

"What about you? What's your type? One of them?" I ask, tilting my bottle in the direction of the women.

His eyes peruse them carefully. "Uh, I'm not sure."

Before I can ask anything else, he sits up and rests his arm on the table, his eyes focused on me. "So you said you weren't from here. Why'd you move to Soledad Square?"

There's too much interest in his eyes. "Why did you?" I counter.

He shrugs. "I happened across this town and decided I liked it enough to give it a go."

"Happened across it? How does that happen?"

"I was traveling. Stopped here for a night. One turned to two, two into three. You get it."

I nod. "I see." He's answering without giving much away and it's driving me insane.

"Where did you come from?"

"West coast area," I reply before taking a drink.

"California?"

"Why do people think the west coast consists only of California?"

"Because it's the biggest state. So, Oregon or Washington?"

I shake my head. "You're asking all these questions and I don't even know your name," I lie, needing to change directions.

"Oh." He chuckles. "Kaspian. You can call me Kas."

"I'm Ezra."

"I know who you are."

His tone flips when he says those five words, but I try not to let it get to me. "Stalking me already?"

"Just curious."

"Why?"

"Why were you so interested in me and what I was doing with that woman?"

"I have reasons."

"Care to share?"

I take another gulp of my beer and put it down on the table. "You know, I think I remember seeing you with another girl in town."

15

He leans back. "Oh yeah?"

I nod. "Yeah. She worked at Perfectly Convenient. I go there all the time for my cigarettes."

Kas takes a sip, his eyes never leaving my face. "Smoker, huh? Those aren't good for you."

"I lean into my vices," I reply, before getting back onto the subject of the girl. "I haven't seen her in a while, though."

"Sometimes people move."

I scratch my jaw as I inspect him. "Interesting that you jumped straight to move. She could've quit."

He shrugs. "That too."

"But I'd think I'd see her somewhere in town even if she quit. It's not like it's a big place, and she never brought up the idea of quitting."

"You talked to her quite a bit, huh?"

"Casual conversation during checkout."

"Hmm."

"Saw the two of you having food together sometimes. Figured you were dating."

"Interesting that you'd assume that."

"So you don't know where she disappeared to?"

"Why would I?"

I give him a one shoulder shrug. "Maybe she mentioned something to you. An ex-boyfriend, crazy stalker, you know?"

His lips quirk up slightly on one side. "Nope." Kas finishes his drink and folds his arms on the table. "You into guys at all?"

The rapid change of direction in our conversation nearly gives me whiplash. "What the fuck are you talking about?"

He snorts. "No need to be so offended."

"I'm not, but where the hell did that come from?"

"First of all, you accepted an offer to have a threesome with me and that girl, and that's only after being so concerned with what I was doing that you followed me. It's not such a stretch to think you might find me attractive."

I can't find any words and end up staring at him with what has to be a stupefied look on my face. When he smirks, I break out of my trance. "Threesomes happen all the time where the guys only fuck the girl, so if you were thinking something else, that's on you. Are *you* into guys?"

"Yeah," he answers easily with a shrug.

"Oh."

He rolls his eyes. "Don't get all weird on me. It's not a big deal."

"I couldn't care less, to be honest."

"Good."

And it's true. I'm not a homophobe. The intimate moments people have don't affect my life, so I don't have anything to say about it, but I don't talk about my sex life with strangers. I'm not exactly an open book. If I were, he'd know just how much I'm not against being with men.

After taking another sip of my beer, I realize he's successfully changed the subject from the missing convenience store girl. My whole reason for hanging out with him is to try to understand who he is and figure out what he's doing to these girls and why.

Usually, I'm good at pretending I'm normal. Just another guy in a small town, who doesn't have a murderous monster caged inside him. But with him, I find I'm a little more on guard. Tense. It's because I know he's like me. I know it like I know I'll never truly be able to rehabilitate myself, and if we're even remotely similar, I know I can't trust him. Maybe I can pretend I do.

"Want to take a shot?" I ask him.

He grins. "Sure."

FOUR

Two shots and another drink later, I wonder if he'll loosen up; unfortunately, he seems to be handling the liquor pretty well. I was hoping the fact that I'm only drinking beer and he's been downing Gin and Tonics would lead to him being more intoxicated, and therefore more willing to let some information slip. I've also been taking my beer bottles back to the bar with me when I get another, despite them only being half-empty.

He gets up to go to the bathroom, leaving me with time to sit and think about how I can get some information out of him. He's good at side-stepping any questions I have, but I guess I can't expect him to come out and say, *yeah, I stalk women in my spare time, and kill them when I'm done with them.* Because nothing could get me to admit to what I've done. Though, I feel like I had good reasons. Does he think he does too?

"Hey! I never see you out. What're you up to?"

I look up and find Willow Bixby in front of my table. She's the receptionist of the landscaping company I work at. She's the pretty face people see when they first come in, and the sultry voice they hear when they call to schedule work. She's probably the nicest person I've met in this town, which is saying a lot, because this town is ripe with do-gooders. It's weird.

"Just having a drink," I reply, holding up my beer.

"I guess that makes sense," she says with a laugh, her cheeks pinking up slightly as she tucks a curly lock of hair behind her ear. "I'm surprised to see you." Her eyes dance over as much of my body as she can see. "I only ever see you in coveralls before you head out to perfect the lawns of our community."

I grin. "That's better than calling me a grass cutter."

"Oh stop. It's more than that and you know it. To design the layout of people's yards, trim the trees and shrubbery, and..." She trails off, perhaps realizing it doesn't sound glamorous at all. "Well, it may not sound like much, but you get things to grow. You bring life to people's homes and public spaces, and you make it look so beautiful."

Too bad bringing plants to life isn't as thrilling as taking a life. Guess I can't say that, though.

"I do my best," I say with a smile. "You here with anyone?"

She turns and jerks her thumb over her shoulder. "My friends are back there somewhere. I guess I should get back to them."

I nod. "Okay. I'll see you on Monday."

"Yep," she replies with a smile before turning away and disappearing into a small group of women.

"Brought you another beer," Kaspian says, appearing out of nowhere shortly after Willow left.

"Thanks. Did you get another drink, too?" Because it appears he's trying to get me drunk.

"I took a shot at the bar."

Don't believe that.

"So, where do you live?" I ask.

His brow lifts and a flirty smile crosses his face. "Want me to take you home, or what?"

I level him with a look. "No, that's not what I mean. Just a question."

"Not really, though. If you want to get to know me, you might ask what my favorite food is, or my favorite sports team. You'd ask about my family or—"

"Family. That's a good one," I cut in.

He stiffens slightly before he says, "What do you want to know?"

I shrug. "Anything. Do you come from a normal family or a dysfunctional one? Are your parents married still? Siblings?"

"Feels like we're dating," he says with a smirk.

"Look, you asked me to hang out. I'm trying to fill the silence. I could just go home."

"Okay, okay. Fine. You're so hostile, Ezra."

I begin to shift out of the bench seat but his voice stops me.

"Parents are still married. It's been about thirty-five years now. They're sickeningly happy and in love after all this time. My sister is older than me by two years but acts like it's ten."

"Sounds...normal." *Too normal. Too perfect. It's a lie.*

He chuckles. "Yeah, I guess. And you? I'm gonna assume dysfunctional."

"Why do you assume that?"

"You give off the *my-family-is-fucked-up* vibe."

"Not sure how to take that."

He shrugs, pushing up the sleeves of his shirt, showing off the ink on both arms.

21

"You the black sheep of your perfect family with all that ink?"

My eyes try to decipher something from the art, but it's all random. A chess board, some skulls, a couple different birds, numbers, a woman.

"I guess so, but they love me regardless of how I choose to decorate my body."

"They love you even though you like men?"

He freezes and the air around us becomes charged. His jaw clenches and his eyes penetrate mine for what feels like a full minute. I pushed a button.

"Yeah," he answers finally. "They don't care."

Another lie. He's either never told them or they don't approve.

"Cool."

"And you? Your family?"

"You were right," I tell him. "Pretty fucked up. I don't know where they are. I don't keep in touch."

"Maybe that's better."

"Maybe."

AFTER DRINKING half of my beer, I get up and tell him I'm going to pay my tab. It's only ten-thirty, but he's not giving me any information I'm interested in, and I'm already peopled out. More and more keep coming in, getting louder, and there's one guy in particular who keeps looking at me in a way I don't like. Before I'm tempted to do something about it, I need to leave.

The bartender rushes over after I've waited near the register for a few minutes. "Sorry, man. What can I get ya?"

"Just paying my tab." I pause. "My friend's too. He's the one that's been drinking Gin and Tonics all night."

His brows furrow slightly as he goes to the register and sifts through the cards. "You're Ezra, right?"

"Yep."

"Who's your friend?"

"Kaspian." I glance back at the booth where Kas sits, eyeing the table of women in front of him. "That one over there."

"Oh. He was drinking a mix of Sprite and water."

That fucker.

"Right. He started with a Gin and Tonic."

"Cool. One second and I'll get you squared away."

Once I pay the bill, I head back to the booth with his card in hand and drop it to the table. "I paid your tab."

His eyes slowly lift and meet mine. "Oh?" He takes his card and flips it back and forth. "Good thing I wasn't lying about my name. Bartenders just give people's cards to strangers? It's a good thing you're not a thief."

Worse.

"This is a small town. Safe. People trust everyone here."

"They probably shouldn't," he says with a glint in his eye.

"No, they probably shouldn't." His eyes flicker past me, probably to his next victim. "I'm going to take a piss then I'm gonna head home."

"Already?"

"Yeah." I don't elaborate on why. It's not like we're friends. I just walk away.

I deliberately take my time, hoping he thinks I've left, and when I emerge back into the darkened room, I'm glad I did. He's got two people sitting in the booth with him. One I can see clearly. She's his typical victim—blonde, young, average. The other person is hidden behind the back of the booth, but I see Kas and the blonde look across the table and smile. A dainty hand reaches for a glass, and it's the only reason I know it's not a guy.

I linger near the hall to the bathrooms, watching him while he works. He's a different person than he was a few minutes ago. He's loose and at ease. He laughs, tilting his head back like whatever was just said was the funniest thing he's ever heard. He covers his face with his tattooed hand as if he's hiding a blush.

God, he's good.

The blonde is smitten already. She looks at him like he's a god. Like she can't wait for him to make her worship him.

I wonder briefly what might happen to this woman. Will she end up disappearing without a trace, too? Should I lurk in the shadows and wait for them to leave? Maybe he's just hoping for a hookup. After watching for another minute, I decide to let whatever's going to happen, happen.

The only way I'll be able to find out more is by letting him believe we're friends.

I t's early October, so the grass isn't growing as quickly. The company I work for—Escape into Nature —has us doing some edging, winter lawn prep, and gearing up for what's always a busy season. Snow removal and plowing is probably the most important job around here between November and March.

As I finish my workday, ready to head home and take a shower, I can't help but wonder what sort of a job Kaspian has. He's really good at wearing the skin of someone normal, maybe better than me. I fucking hate to admit that, but I'm curious if he works with people or stays away from them. I'm guessing the former.

You may question why I care, and I couldn't tell you. Like I said before, he's intriguing. I've never liked *open book* people. They tell you everything you need to know about them in your first twenty-minute conversation. Kaspian's good at pivoting away from questions. When he answers them, I don't believe most of what he says. You'd think that would be annoying, but not to me. All that means is that he's got something to hide, and it makes me want to dig deeper and find it out.

I've always wondered why I am the way that I am. The way media calls it is that you grew up in a fucked up family and dealt with abuse. Maybe your father beat your mom. Maybe your mom beat you. Perhaps they were druggies and alcoholics who brought home whores and pimps and fucked them in front of you. And perhaps you watched them die.

But what if you grew up in a fairly wealthy neighborhood? What if you were never hit, never starved, and never neglected? What if you had absolutely everything going for you and yet you still had these urges? Dark and demanding.

I can't diagnose myself. I can't really pin it on one particular thing. Is it a mental illness? Was I born with something missing? I've read that genetics can play a part, and a person's environment can possibly trigger that thing in your brain that turns you into a monster.

I want to study Kaspian. I want to know about his past, his life, and why he does the things he does. I know I don't have proof, but I feel it deep inside my fucking bones. I know he's killing these women, and maybe, just maybe, I can get that high from the mere knowledge of his crimes. Maybe he'll fill me in on the details or maybe I'll be able to watch and it'll keep me from doing what I've been dying to do for two years.

ONCE I'M HOME, showered, and changed, I nuke some baked ziti in the microwave. As I wait for it to be done, I lean against the kitchen counter and reach for my phone on the other side of the sink. It slips from my fingers and careens into a water and soap-filled casserole dish that was soaking in the sink. I'm quick to retrieve it, snatching a gray towel from the handle of the oven to dry it off. I immediately test it out to see if it works, happy to see that it unlocks and comes on with no issues. I tap the internet icon and breathe a sigh of relief when the page comes up.

The microwave dings, so I remove my food, grab a fork, and take it to the living room before going back to the kitchen for a bottle of Coke and my phone. When I sit down and click on a video to watch, the sound is muffled.

"Fuck."

I try a couple different videos and they all sound the same. The speakers are messed up. As I continue to play with it, it shuts off on its own.

With a sigh, I throw it to the cushion next to me and plan to visit my cell phone provider with the hope that it's a quick and easy fix.

Luckily, in a town this size, nothing is ever too far away. I've chosen to live on the outer edge of town, away from the business district, far from people. So it's a little out of the way, but it still doesn't take long to get there.

When I step into the brightly lit room, besides the dozens of phones taking up space, there's also a dozen fucking people in here. I think it might be time for this town to open up another store, but what do I know?

I get in line and do my best to drown out the voice of an annoying teenage girl begging her mom for a brand new phone, the toddler throwing a fit on the floor, and a couple quietly arguing over an ex who sent a text.

The line moves slowly, and the bell rings behind me, alerting everyone that yet another person is here to take up space. One of the employees raises his hand and says, "Can you open up over there?" He points to an unmanned desk, so I guess it's another worker.

When I spot the worker making his way to the left of me, I barely glance over, but I glimpse some familiar ink.

My eyes slowly travel up his arms until I lock onto his face. It's him all right. Great, now he'll think I'm stalking him.

As he does some stuff on the computer, two people in front of me move forward, so when he raises his head to grab the next customer, he sees that it's me.

His lips curl up slowly. "Sir, I can help you here."

I stroll up to his counter and push my phone across. "I dropped it in water. The speakers don't seem to be working right, and then it turned off."

"You didn't turn it off right away?" he asks, handling the phone.

"Was I supposed to?"

He laughs. "Did you put it in rice?"

"Are you gonna keep asking me questions or actually try to fix it?"

"Do you want to upgrade? This phone looks pretty old. Is this the original?"

I stare at him. "I don't need to get a new phone every time one comes out."

"Yeah, but we've had like six come out since this one."

Annoyed, I snatch the phone from his hand. "Fine. I'll go see someone else."

His hand is on mine in a nanosecond, trapping the phone between my fingers as he squeezes my hand tightly. "No, you won't. I'll take care of you."

As he releases his grip, he takes my phone back, working quietly to take it apart. He removes the battery, replaces it with a new one he retrieved from the back, and attempts to turn it back on. I watch his fingers work, curious as to what they do in their free time. Does he strangle these women? I bet he does. I don't see him using a gun. Too messy and too loud. A knife is typically personal, and he doesn't seem to have a history with these women. He suffocates them in some way, watching them struggle. I can tell that's the kind of sicko he is.

When I realize his hands have stopped moving, my eyes flicker up and find he's watching me with the tiniest grin on his face.

"You're gonna have to leave it here to get worked on. We can send it out tonight. It has more damage than I hoped. It's probably because it's so fucking old."

"And in the meantime, I don't have a phone?"

"We can set you up with a flip phone."

"A flip phone," I repeat.

He smirks. "It's not much worse than this," he says, holding up my ruined one.

"Fine."

We spend another ten minutes getting my information down, transferring my number to the temp phone, and then he lets me know I'll get a call in a week or so.

"What're you doing this weekend?" he asks before I walk away.

"Nothing."

"Want to hit up this club? It's in the next town over, but it's nice."

"I'm not really a club person."

"Yeah, I can see that," he says. "Well, what do you do for fun?"

"Not much."

"You act like you're sixty. How old are you?"

"Thirty."

"Ah, an older man. I've always liked them a bit older."

Is he flirting with me?

"What are you doing?"

He grins. "I'm twenty-three, so you're not that much older."

"I didn't ask." But it's information I tuck away anyway.

"You wanted to know."

I hate him.

"Okay, well, thanks for talking shit about my phone, calling me old, and not really helping me at all."

I turn and walk away, and I make it two steps outside before the door opens. "Sir," he says, putting on a show for anyone listening. "My card." He slips the cardstock in my hand, his fingers brushing against mine. "Call me if you need help with the new phone, or," his eyes lock onto mine for a few seconds, "anything else."

I take the card and shove it in my pocket before walking to my car.

CHAPTER
SIX

Eight days go by and I still haven't heard back about my phone. I know it might take a while, but just like everyone else in this fucking world, I've become attached to it. I regularly reach into my pocket just to pull out a flip phone that doesn't offer me the ability to check the weather, news, or email.

I've caught a few glimpses of Kaspian here and there, but we haven't talked, and I've yet to see him with another girl. I wonder if he did anything with the one from the bar. Does he keep them alive awhile before disposing of them? Maybe he's been preoccupied with one.

"Hey, Ezra. What can I get you today?" Shevon asks as she approaches my table at Thai Me Down—a, you guessed it, Thai restaurant.

"Let me get the pineapple fried rice and fried prawns."

"You want anything else to drink besides water?"

"No, I'm good. Thanks, Shevon."

She smiles and nods, walking away.

I never thought I'd be one of those people who live in a

town where you become a regular at almost every business. Where people know your name and you know theirs. These types of towns are known for being gossipy. Everybody knows what everybody else is doing. Take for example, Kathy and Bill over there. I know Bill's cheating on Kathy. Kathy knows too. She hates him for it, but she won't leave him simply because she won't give him up to the other woman. Marco in the corner is struggling with addiction to painkillers. His mom kicks him out of her house at least twice a month. Jeremiah sits near the window, his laptop open, probably doing some schoolwork. He was just accepted into Dartmouth, and his mom tells everyone she comes across.

What do people say about me, I wonder?

When Shevon returns with my food, she places the plates in front of me before cocking her hip and crossing her arms. "So, I heard Jimmy from the theater took off. Up and left town. Didn't even tell his girlfriend. Ain't that some shit?"

See?

"Really?" I ask, needing to fit in. Needing to pretend. "That's weird, isn't it? Why would someone just run away?"

Shevon's head swivels around, her shoulder-length curly hair bouncing with the move. Her voice lowers to a whisper. "People who run away like this have to be running from something. He must've done something bad."

"Like what?"

"Heard he got caught with some seventeen-year-old girl at the theater."

My eyes widen. "Are you serious?"

She nods. "He's disgusting. I've always had a weird feeling about him."

32

"Damn."

"I say good riddance. We don't need people like that in this town. I hope he gets what's coming to him."

I nod along. "Me too."

She rushes off, but when she comes back with some more water, she lingers again. "Poor Kathy. I don't know why she puts up with Bill and his shit." I shrug, and she leans in to whisper again. "Maybe she's planning on killing him."

Shevon covers her mouth when she laughs. "I shouldn't say that. That's awful."

I grin. "It's okay. I won't say anything." I give her a wink and reach for my glass.

"Why are you single, again?" she asks.

This isn't the first time she's questioned me. Shevon is beautiful. She's tall, slender, and has gorgeous brown skin and a bright smile. She could be a model in any magazine and on any runway. I've sensed she's wanted me to ask her out, but it's not personal. If I was normal, I'd be crazy to ignore her, but she's too pure to deal with my shit.

"I'm a handful," I say with a chuckle. "I'm sparing everyone."

She playfully smacks my shoulder. "Oh, stop."

The bell above the door rings and Shevon turns around. "Oh, speaking of single. Since you won't take me out, I think I'm gonna try my chances on him."

I peek around her and spot Kaspian.

"Please don't."

She gives me a look like she thinks I'm jealous. "Well, if you want to stop me..." She wiggles her brows.

"What do you know about him?" I ask.

"That he's hot as fuck. You know it's those skinny ones

you gotta watch out for. If you know what I'm saying," she says, dropping her voice and giving me a pointed look.

"I have no idea what you're saying."

I do, though.

She laughs. "Anyway, I don't know much. He's kind of new. Not too new, but you know. Someone said he moved here from Maine and someone else said Massachusetts. Now, either people are confused by those two M states, or he's telling people different stories. My friend tried talking to him once. She said he was nice, but quiet. This guy I know said he was pretty rude to him, and the complete opposite of nice and quiet. Terrance told me he thinks he might be gay, because he saw him extremely close to a guy once, but I've seen him with a few girls, so I don't know. He's kind of an enigma."

Yeah, and I want to be the one to figure him out.

"I see."

Kaspian spots me and lifts his hand.

"You know him?" Shevon asks, her eyebrows jumping to her hairline.

"I wouldn't say that. I took my phone into the shop last week and he works there. I may have seen him around town, but..."

I trail off as I notice him walking this way. Shevon steps back and her eyes bounce between us a couple times before she faces Kaspian.

"Hi. You sittin' here?"

Kas glances at me, waiting. I give a quick nod.

"Sure," he says with a smile.

"Can I get you something to drink? Water? Coke? Sprite?"

"Water is fine, and whatever this rice is he has. I'll take that. Thanks."

She gives me another look, wondering why someone I don't really know would sit with me. Great. Now I look like a liar, but I really don't fucking know this guy. Not well. Not as much as I wish I did.

"News on my phone?"

"You using me, Ezra?" he asks with a good-natured smile. "Just want me for my skills and not my friendship?"

"I don't *want* you for anything. I just want my phone."

He sits back, his body relaxed as he stretches his leg under the table, his knee bumping into mine. "Oh, come on. You don't have to lie."

"What are you talking about?" I ask before shoveling a forkful of rice in my mouth.

"It doesn't matter," he says, leaning to his side and pulling my phone from his pocket. He slides it across the table. "There you go. Special delivery."

"You do this for everyone in town? Track them down and give them their phones?"

"Only the special ones," he says with a smile. "I still think you should upgrade, but whatever. You got the other phone on you?"

I pick it up from the bench beside me and happily toss it over. "I don't know why those phones still exist."

He chuckles. "I already switched service over."

"What if I needed to make a call and it didn't work?" I ask, staring at him.

"Who would you call? You don't have friends."

"What makes you think that? I know plenty of people."

"Knowing people and being friends with people are two different things." He pauses. "So, why didn't you call me? I gave you my number. Figured I'd hear from you."

"What would I say?"

"Wow, you really don't know how to talk to people, do you?"

"I do, actually. I function just fine. It's you—" I cut myself off, not wanting to finish what I was going to say.

"It's me what?" he questions, leaning in. "You don't know how to talk to me? Why?"

Luckily, Shevon is back with his food. "Here you go. I hope you enjoy."

"Thank you."

We eat in silence for a few minutes before he speaks up.

"*Tie* me down."

My brows furrow as I look up and meet his gaze. "Excuse me?"

His lips twitch. "The restaurant name."

"Oh. Yeah."

"Kinky, right? But I like it. Do you have any kinks?"

He's so rapid-fire, it's hard to keep up. He jumps from one topic to another like it's nothing. And he's been flirting with me. Is this flirting? Girls flirt differently than guys, and with them, I can usually tell. I've dealt with men a couple times, but Kaspian is different. He's different from anyone I've ever met, so I'm not sure if he's just nosy, or if he's trying to rile me up, or if he's flirting.

He asked what my kinks are, he asked if I was into guys, he grabbed my hand rather possessively in the store , telling me he'd take care of me. And his knee is still touching mine under the table.

"My kink is silence. It really gets me going."

He snorts, but then mimes locking his lips closed before throwing away the invisible key. I roll my eyes as my mouth begins to form a smile.

His eyes light up a bit, but he doesn't say anything.

36

Surprisingly, we finish our food without a word being spoken.

Shevon comes back to drop off our checks, but before I can reach for mine, Kaspian snatches it up. When I look at him, he puts his finger to his lips like he's telling me to be quiet, and when Shevon walks by, he hands her both tickets with his card.

"You didn't have to pay," I tell him.

"Are we talking now?"

"Why are you such a pain in the ass?"

"I guess it's my kink. To annoy people."

I shake my head. "You're good at it."

"I'm quite good at a lot. Did you know silence kink is a thing? Were you being serious or just trying to get me to shut up?"

"Maybe both."

"It's used in BDSM. The submissive is to remain silent, and if they don't, the dominant can dish out punishment. It's also used in slave training."

"That's nice."

"Are you a dominant?" he questions. "Into BDSM at all?"

"Why do you want to know? Do you want to submit to me?"

His head tilts to the side as his brows lift, like he's surprised and considering it. "Might be fun. Not gonna lie," he says with a laugh. "But I'm into guys. You haven't really said."

Shevon brings his card back. "Thanks guys. Have a good night."

I stand up and put on my jacket before heading to the door.

Leaving Thai Me Down, I shove my hands in my pockets

and walk around the corner of the restaurant, heading down Fifth Street and away from the main road.

"Did you park back here?" Kaspian asks, jogging to catch up. "So, I wanted to ask if you wanted to go out this weekend? Not on a date, since you still haven't said whether you like guys or not. I mean, even if you did, I guess that doesn't mean you have to like me, I'm just assuming...Anyway, I'm getting off track. That club I told you about. Well, okay, maybe it's a little kinky, but I think it would be fun."

I whirl around and push him into a narrow alleyway, shoving him against the brick wall of the restaurant we were just in. My hand is on his chest, my left foot between his feet as I push in close. His eyes show his surprise as they widen.

"What the fuck are you doing?"

His chest heaves, but he doesn't attempt to push me back or move at all. "What do you mean?"

"You and this constant flirting you're doing. Getting me to go to kink clubs with you? You think that's what I want to do?"

"How would I know if I didn't ask?" he counters, straightening his back.

My hand slides up to his throat, my fingers digging into his skin. I've never been into strangulation, but there's definitely something intimate about it. His pulse races under my touch, his dark eyes stare into mine, and his breath dances across the back of my hand. To be this close, to be able to take my time if I wanted to...to feel the last breaths leaving someone's body...it's much different than a quick knife to the heart.

What Kaspian doesn't offer me, and what I've enjoyed previously, is the begging. He's not pleading for his life.

38

He's not even struggling. Maybe it's because I'm not really trying to kill him. I don't want him dead. Not yet anyway. I have more to learn.

His hand comes to rest on my wrist, his round eyes watching me carefully, like I'm an animal that could sink my teeth into him at any second.

"You gonna kill me?" he asks. "Because I invited you out?" I don't respond, instead my grip tightens. "If you're not interested, just say that," he rasps. "But remember, you followed me. Tell me why."

With another shove, I release his throat and take a step back. His fingertips brush against his Adam's apple, but he continues to wait for an answer.

"Why a kink club?" I ask instead.

"I like submissive women," he answers easily. "And dominant men." He takes a step forward. "What do you like?"

My eyes roam his face—the small amount of hair covering his jaw, the thin nose ring attached to his perfectly shaped nose, and his brown eyes surrounded by long, dark lashes. He's attractive and admitting that isn't startling to me. Beautiful people exist in the world, both men and women. My experience with them is unbalanced to say the least, but that doesn't mean I'm completely inexperienced.

Kaspian is the first man to make me feel so many different things, though. Confused, worried, annoyed, angry, and intrigued.

I'm not hesitant because we're both men. I'm hesitant because he's a stalker and a murderer, and how can two killers be anything but enemies? You don't trust a murderer. You can't. But there's a tiny part of me that wonders if we can be friends. Who's gonna admit to what they do first, though? The fact that we've been getting away with our crimes shows we're pretty good at keeping shit to ourselves.

I shake my head. "I don't know."

His smile spreads slowly across his lips, the corners of his mouth pulling upwards. "I think that's the first time you've been honest with me."

SEVEN

I never thought I'd be here—dressed in black slacks and a black button up, walking into a fetish club with Kaspian at my side. Apparently black is part of the dress code. No jeans or T-shirts allowed.

"It's couples' night," Kas tells me right before we approach the man just past the door.

"What?"

"Shh. Hey, Nick." He greets the bald man like he knows him fairly well. Maybe he does.

"Kaspian," the man says in response. "Signing him in?"

"Yep. Give him your ID," he tells me.

I pass it along, and after some quick paperwork in which I have to look over the rules, the man glances at Kas. "You know you're responsible for him."

"I do."

The man gives me a look that tells me not to do anything stupid, but he doesn't say anything as he hands my ID back.

"So, you come here often," I say to Kas as we move past the hulking figure and through a narrow hall.

"I wouldn't say *often*, but..." he trails off with a shrug and leads me to a bar.

I wasn't sure what to expect, but so far it's fairly normal. The area around the bar is typical of any local hangout. There's tables and chairs, a pool table, and plenty of people interacting. The room is dim with purple hues illuminating from various locations—above the bar, on the walls, and under tables.

"Here you go," Kaspian says, handing me a drink.

"Is it Gin and Tonic or Sprite?" I ask.

He smirks. "Guess you'll have to have a taste."

After a sip, I find that it's a vodka soda. "You drinking the same or you trying to get me drunk while you stay sober?"

Kaspian laughs. "You'll appreciate the alcohol in a little while."

We find two empty stools near the end of the bar and make ourselves comfortable. Kaspian's eyes flicker around the room, and I wonder if he's looking for someone to approach. Isn't that how it works? You just ask someone if they wanna sleep with you?

"Where do people fuck in here?" I ask.

"Anxious already?" he asks in a teasing tone.

"Just curious."

"There's another area. I'm just easing you in. Drink up."

As I take the final sip of my drink, a man walks up and instantly grabs the attention of everyone in the vicinity. He's wearing black leather pants and a black zip-up vest that goes up to his neck and fits snug against his body. His bare arms are cut but lean, his skin like porcelain. He has a shaved head and soft features, dancing between both feminine and masculine.

"Master Blake," Kaspian says, standing up to shake his hand.

"Kaspian. Nice to see you again."

"Yeah, I figured I'd show my face around here since it's been a while."

The man gives a barely perceptible smirk. "And who's this? New boyfriend?"

Before I can say anything, Kas lays a hand on my shoulder, giving me a slight squeeze. "Yes. It's new."

"Throwing him into the deep end right off the bat, huh?"

Kas chuckles. "Something tells me he can handle it."

Master Blake extends his hand to me, so I take it. His shake is firm and his gaze is penetrating. He stares at me like he knows every secret I've ever had. "Nice to meet you..."

"Ezra," I say.

"Ezra. I hope you enjoy yourself."

"Thanks."

Kas sits back down and orders us a shot to go with another drink. "Master Blake runs this place."

"Seems like it," I say. "Your type?"

He gives me a lopsided grin that makes me regret asking, because I know what's coming.

"Jealous?"

"No."

"I don't have a type," he offers. "I'm an equal opportunist."

"I see."

We down our shots and start on our second drink of the night. A couple who appear to be in their forties approach us with friendly smiles.

"How are you two tonight?" the woman asks.

43

"We're great. How are you?" Kas responds in a cheerful tone.

"We're doing pretty good." The man wraps an arm around his wife's waist and grins. "We were wondering if you two were interested in joining us tonight."

My eyebrows lift, but Kas is quick. He reaches out and grabs my hand and the touch has me tensing up. He gently rubs his thumb over the back of my hand, telling me to calm down.

"Thank you for thinking of us, but we're gonna have to decline. My guy here is still a little new."

The couple look in my direction and give me a head tilt and smile. "I see. Well, good luck and have a good night."

"You too."

As soon as they're gone, Kas removes his hand.

"That was...new," I say, watching the couple walk away.

"It's what this place is for."

"They accepted the rejection well."

"Everyone here does. No means no."

He slaps me on the back. "Okay, you've had enough to drink. Let's wander."

The alcohol does have me feeling a little looser, so I follow him with no questions, and then we get to a hall lined with doors leading to private rooms. Some have windows for people to watch. Kas stops in front of one and jerks his head, telling me to look.

Inside, a man fucks a woman from behind while holding onto a chain that's connected to a leather collar around her throat.

"Damn," I whisper.

We watch for a few more minutes before moving down the hall.

"These are group rooms," Kas says, walking inside one.

There are a couple black leather couches alongside two walls, and three large beds taking up the rest of the space. On one couch, a man is riding another man, his hand on his cock as he seeks a release. One of the beds hold two men and one woman while another man watches from nearby.

"That could've been us," Kas whispers into my ear, his breath tickling my flesh. "When you followed me to my hotel room."

Our eyes meet and we're frozen in time for several seconds.

"Too bad your girl left you."

His gaze drops to my mouth briefly before looking up again. "She didn't leave me and she wasn't mine."

"Did you get rid of her when you noticed me following you?" I ask, needing to know.

"Why would I do that?" he questions, his voice a whisper.

The woman with the two men screams when she climaxes, stealing our attention. She climbs off the blond man's lap, and then the Black guy drops to his knees between the guy's legs and licks the woman's juices from his dick. My cock hardens, which I suppose is normal for a place like this, but I fear it'll never go down if we keep watching people have sex.

"Why did you have a hotel room?" I ask him, trying to get back on track.

"I don't like people at my house."

"So anytime you fuck someone, you rent a hotel room?"

"Or I go to theirs."

"Hmm."

He watches me for a few seconds, waiting for me to say something else. Maybe he's waiting for more. When I don't

45

do anything but gaze back at the men on the couch, he clears his throat. "I'll be back."

I don't have time to ask where he's going before he's already out of the room, leaving me leaning against a wall, watching everyone do what I wish I could be doing right now.

It isn't until I notice one of the workers cleaning the couch that was just used that I even realize Kaspian's been gone for a little while. I walk out, my head swiveling from side to side, trying to determine which way to go.

I don't find Kaspian lingering in any other group rooms, and I end up back at the bar, ordering another shot. A couple approaches me, asking where my partner is since it's couples only night and singles aren't supposed to be here. I tell them he's in the bathroom, and they tell me to find them once I have him if we're interested in some fun.

I ask someone where the bathrooms are, but I don't find Kas there. Anger starts coursing through my veins along with the liquor. Why would he bring me here just to leave me? We're not even in town, so it's not like I can just walk home. We're an hour away from Soledad Square, and his absence is starting to piss me off.

Traveling back through a hall of private rooms, I make a turn and head to the group room we were in before. Maybe he went back looking for me. When I don't see him, I storm back through the hall, ready to go outside and call an Uber, but something catches my eye.

Black leather and ink. More specifically, a man decked in black leather pushing up against Kaspian, and his inked arms held above his head against the wall.

I stop and watch.

The man leans in, whispering something in Kaspian's ear, but he's blocking his face and I can't see his reaction. I can't imagine he's in this position against his will. Kas wouldn't let this happen if he didn't want it to, and like he said earlier, no means no. If he didn't want this, it wouldn't be happening, but it is.

They're in a private room, but the door remains open. A couple of other people peek in but move on quickly. I, however, continue to stand in the doorway.

Eventually, Kaspian's hands are released, but they quickly find another home running down the large man's back. They travel lower and lower, until they curve around his waist.

My heart beats faster and harder. I don't know if I'm angry or turned on. Maybe both.

When Kaspian's hand reaches for what's between the man's legs, he shifts, and his eyes find mine over the other guy's shoulder.

His arms drop to his sides and he whispers something. The man turns around, his ice blue eyes surveying me.

"Hey," Kas says to me. "Can you give us a minute?" he asks the man.

A brief pause. "Sure. I'll go find Lex," he states, presumably referring to his partner.

He saunters toward me, his eyes never leaving mine. I don't bother to make room for him through the doorway, forcing him to shift to the side and shimmy through.

Kaspian is quiet for a while. "Sorry, I just wanted—"

"Wanted what?" I ask, stepping inside and closing the door before leaning against it, my arms crossed in front of me.

Kas steps away from the wall opposite me, coming my way. "It doesn't matter. You want to go?"

"No. I want you to tell me what you wanted."

He's only a foot away, watching me with something akin to guilt in his eyes. Maybe shame.

"What do you think? We're in a fucking sex club."

"If you wanted to fuck someone here, why did you even bring me?"

He gives me a look like I should know why. He finally sighs and gives me a one-shoulder shrug. "It's couples' night. I needed someone to come with me."

"So you used me."

The door behind me pushes open, so I step aside and look to see who it is. It's fucking Blue Eyes.

"Hey Kas. I wanted to see if you—"

"He's fine. He's here with me," I say, shoving the door closed.

Kaspian raises an eyebrow at me. "He's watching through the window."

I step toward him, pinning him against the wall with my body. "This is what you want? A guy to trap you against a wall?"

He peers up at me through dark lashes, a hint of a smile on his lips. "Amongst other things."

I bring my hand to his throat, my thumb brushing against his chin. His teeth sink into his bottom lip. "We have an audience."

"Good, because if they weren't here, I don't know what I'd do to you."

He makes a noise in the back of his throat. "What do you mean?"

"You pissed me off."

"Hmm. And you don't like that."

"No. I don't."

He arches his hips and his cock pushes into mine. "Feels like you like it a little."

48

"Don't use me again. For any reason. Especially if you're just going to disappear to get your dick touched."

He nods once. "So, you do like guys," he says, his hand coming between us, his knuckles brushing my growing erection.

"I wouldn't say that."

He smirks. "So, you like me."

"I wouldn't say that either."

His fingers undo my pants and slowly dip into the waistband of my boxer-briefs. He pauses, waiting for me to stop him.

Maybe it's the liquor, or perhaps it's all the sexual energy in this place. I've watched people fuck in multiple ways since being here, and it would be a lie to say it didn't affect me. I'm definitely turned on, so I let him put his hand on me. His fingers wrap around my shaft, and he moans.

"Mm."

I close my eyes while he touches me.

"Look at me," he says. I don't. He strokes a few more times. "Look at me." I don't listen. "I did get rid of the girl when I saw you following me," he whispers.

My eyes fly open. "Why?"

"Because my plan worked."

He runs his thumb over my crown and it takes everything in me to ask another question, because all I want to do is succumb to the pleasure his touch is giving me.

"What plan?"

He runs his nose up the side of my neck until his lips brush against the shell of my ear. His breath dances across my flesh when he says, "To get your attention."

KASPIAN

He pulls away quicker than I was ready for, shoving his cock back in his pants and fastening them back up.

"What are you talking about?" His brows furrow, creating deep lines between them.

"Maybe right now isn't the best time to talk about this."

"Are you saying you were taking these girls solely to get my attention?"

"*Taking*?" I question.

"Enough with the games, Kaspian."

"That's funny, coming from you."

"Me?"

"That's right. You."

He huffs before turning and leaving. I'm quick on his heels, following him through the building until we're outside. Ezra cuts to the right, but there's nothing out here. The club is miles from another business or residence. It's secluded on purpose.

"Where are you going?" I ask.

He ignores me and keeps walking, so I turn back and

head for the car. He's not gonna make it very far, and I'm good at tracking people, so I'll find him.

Two minutes later, I pull up alongside him on a narrow road that'll lead us to the highway. After I push the button to bring the window down, I say, "Just get in."

"Fuck you."

"Well, I thought that's where we were headed."

He doesn't have anything to say to that, so when he keeps walking, I pull over as far into the grass as I can and get out.

"We've dragged this out long enough," I tell him. "I know who you are."

His steps come to a halt and he spins around. "And who is that?"

"It's definitely not Ezra Hamilton, as you'd have everybody in Soledad Square believe."

He doesn't say anything, unwilling to confess. Which I get. It's what we've been doing since we met. We both know more about each other than we'd like to believe, but until now, we've only danced around that fact.

"Why did they call you Heart Stopper?"

He's silent, his eyes focused on me as his jaw ticks. I realize I'm probably standing too close to be lobbing such accusations, but I'm not about to show him any fear now. As he stands, illuminated by my headlights, the trees tall and looming behind him, I feel like I'm in a horror movie. His fists are balled at his sides, and then he takes a step toward me.

I almost move backward, but stand my ground. When he's toe to toe with me, he brings his arm up, pushing up the sleeve to reveal a black bracelet. With a squeeze to the side of the rectangular metal clasp, the bracelet comes apart, and I realize it's not just a bracelet. It's a knife. The blade is just over an inch, but it's sharp, and in the right spot it can get the job done.

Ezra drags the tip of the blade down my chest, stopping at my heart. "Because I always pierce the heart. His other hand comes up, his fingers pressing against my ribs. "One, two, three, four." He counts them quietly, watching my face. "Right here," he says, pressing hard between two of my ribs. "You gotta angle it right and have a long enough blade that's also thin enough to fit between the ribs. But with some practice, you can penetrate the left ventricle. Heart Stopper is both catchy and accurate, though any murderer stops the heart.

"Fortunately for you, this blade I have now is way too small to reach your heart." He pulls it away from my ribs and brings it closer to my neck. "But I'm finding a new thrill in this right here," he says, pushing it flat against my carotid artery. "Feeling the blood pump under my hand, aware that one cut would split the skin and that beautiful crimson liquid would pour out. The warmth of it would coat my fingers and run down my wrist in rivulets." He inhales deeply, the tip of the blade pricking my neck. "Knowing I could end your life if I wanted to."

"But you don't want to," I say softly.

He looks down at me, only two inches taller, but now that I know, and now that he's confessed, his whole demeanor has changed. He seems larger than he is. Harder. Colder. His face is chiseled, sharp lines at his jaw and cheekbones. He's almost transformed into a different person, and now as he peers down at me, fear prickles along my arms for the first time.

His deep-set brown eyes narrow under his brows, his nearly proportionate lips coming together as he clenches his jaw. It feels like he stares at me for hours, the silence growing around us.

"How do you know who I am?"

"Because I'm a hunter."

"I'd say stalker."

"I wouldn't."

"And you hunt...who? Killers? Not the smartest thing to do."

"No, not killers. Not until you, anyway."

He rubs a thumb across his bottom lip, glancing to the side before aiming his penetrating gaze at me again. "I'm gonna need more information, because if you know who I am, then you're a threat, and I have a certain way of handling threats."

I step back. "I'm not going to say anything. Let's go talk."

"At your house," he says, giving me a look that says there isn't another option.

"Explain," he says as soon as his ass hits my couch.

"Uh, okay." I sit down in the armchair to his left, but his eyes are bouncing around the room, looking for anything he can.

This place holds no personal photos. He won't find pictures of family or childhood friends. He won't find anything that tells him anything about me. It's a modest place. I got it for a really good price because it was in fore-closure. It came with issues, but nothing major. It's a converted barn house surrounded by land and trees.

"I saw you well before you ever spotted me. It was

55

months ago, shortly after I got to town. Something about you drew me in. I watched you. Followed you. Asked people about you. Nobody knew much, and something about that was weird, especially in a town like this, so I did some digging."

"What does that mean? Digging?"

"What most people aren't capable of. I'm pretty tech savvy. There's nothing that ties you to *Ezra Hamilton*. Once I realized that was a fake name, I just had to work a little harder. A background check brought up little information, but there was one thing. You got pulled over for speeding six years ago. Had to go to court. The court record had you as Ezra Black, and Ezra Black lived in Seattle. After more online sleuthing, I found out there wasn't an Ezra Black in Seattle. Well, not one that was under fifty, but there was a Quintin Black, and though most of the photos of Quintin Black were a little old, there was no denying it was you. I'm assuming you thought better of only changing one of your names."

I sit back and stretch my arms over the arm rests.

"You satisfied with yourself?"

I shrug. "A little. It was a lot of work."

"And how did you connect Quintin with the killings?"

"The first two were personal. You had a connection with them both. I'm not sure how the cops didn't figure out you did it."

"Maybe I'm a good liar."

I grin. "Maybe."

"Why did you want my attention? And what exactly were you doing to get it?"

"I saw you watching me, and after the first girl, I saw you a bit more. You think I was at Perfectly Convenient by coincidence? I was there because you went there."

"And the library?"

"You were working the grounds there. I'd hope you'd see me and think to come back."

"The girls?"

"What about them?"

"What do you do with them?"

"Different things. It depends."

"Cryptic."

"Why do you kill people?"

"I haven't in a while."

"Why *did* you kill people? Or more importantly, why did you stop?"

"You do know it's not normal to kill people, right?"

"So you want to be *normal?*"

"I don't want to keep running. I'm finally somewhat settled, with little fear of getting caught. Well, until now." He gives me a pointed look, and I wink at him.

"Where are the girls?" he asks again.

"Why do you care about them?"

"I don't. I want to know why you do."

I sink my teeth into my bottom lip. "So you are interested in me," I tease.

He doesn't respond with an eye roll or a *fuck you*, instead he remains stoic. "I am. I want to know why you're the way you are."

"Do we have to have a reason? What if I like it?"

"You still haven't told me what *it* is."

I take a deep breath. "Well, the Perfectly Convenient girl is dead. She had to go because she started catching on to me being there for you instead of her. I think I asked one too many questions, and she seemed to like you. I couldn't have her telling you anything before I was ready. The library girl is gone too. That was accidental. Well, not really. I accidentally went too far when we were fucking. She got angry and started yelling, but we were at her place and her neighbors are nosy. I had to shut her up quickly, and well..."

"Went too far?" he asks, as if killing her wasn't bad enough.

"I didn't rape her. Jesus. I'm not a monster." I crack a grin at him and he shakes his head. "Too rough," I add with a shrug. "Not everyone likes spankings, I guess."

"She wasn't submissive enough for you?" he bites.

I bypass that. "But I was using them to get your attention. I knew you were watching. I wanted you to be. I'd hope you'd confront me. I know a couple of your kills seemed to be justified. Two men in the suburbs of Seattle beat the living shit out of one of your friends, right? A girl. You were the vigilante hero when justice wasn't served. I figured you had a soft spot for women. I lured you in."

"I don't have a soft spot for women."

"No. Not all of them, huh?" I say with a wink.

"That one in particular was different. She was good to me. Nice. I didn't know her well, but I knew her life wasn't easy. Even with her own problems, she was always offering me help when she thought I was going through a hard time. She got drunk at a party. These guys didn't just beat her. They raped her. They pissed on her. They stole from her."

"I saw. They got off easy. Nobody believed they raped her."

"Of course not. She was a drunk woman at a party. She was asking for it, right?" He shakes his head. "I made sure they paid for it."

I give him a little clap. "And I commend you for it. I can see why the cops wouldn't connect you with her. I found her name and the case, and because everyone is on social media these days, it was easy to find her. She's been posting pictures and statuses for over a decade on Facebook. In all

58

that time, you're only halfway in one picture. Just this," I say, gesturing to the side of my neck down to my collarbone. "You ducked out, but you have a very obvious scar," I say, eyeing it. "When I saw that, and saw how they were killed, I knew it was you. The same person who killed Phillip Davis, Patrick Reeves, and Bernard and Giorgia Black."

I
f he's shocked at how much I know, he doesn't show it. Not even a flinch. But surprising to no one, he doesn't touch on what I just said. He moves on.

"If you used those girls just to get to me, then what about prior?"

"What makes you think I have priors?"

"You're good. Not the best, but you're good. You slip into the skin of a shy, charming guy. You bring your victims to you. You lured me in by luring them in, and you don't learn that overnight." He shifts, scooting to the edge of the couch as he faces me. "I asked about you, too. Everybody gets a different version of you. Some say you're nice, some say you're rude. Somebody says you're from Maine, another person says you're from Massachusetts. You're keeping the truth to yourself and spinning lies to everyone else. The story you told me about your perfect family? It's a lie. I knew it as soon as you said it.

"I'm not extremely tech savvy, but I know a little. I looked into Kaspian Loughton in both Maine and Mass-achusetts. Nothing comes up. No social media accounts either. To be honest, I didn't expect to find anything. You're a different person here than wherever you came from. You have to be. Just like me."

I tilt my head from side to side. "Not bad. There's been a few others. Didn't kill them all though. I guess you can say I have an obsessive personality. Not to be confused with obsessive compulsive disorder, but did you know there's actually a thing called obsessive love disorder?"

"And what is that? The need to be loved and praised every second of the day?"

"Well, who wouldn't want that?" I reply with a smile. "But no, I want the ability to love and praise the person I'm with without being labeled a clingy psycho. Why is it so bad to want to know everything about someone? Why is it a bad thing to want to spend time with them? Why the fuck is it wrong to not want them hanging out and talking to other guys when they're supposed to love me? I mean, really? What is wrong with people?"

My anger rises fast, so I take a breath and try to let it go.

He regards me for several seconds. "I'm going to assume there's a story there. What happened? You fell in love, but she didn't love you back?"

"She said she loved me," I seethe. "She spoke the words over and over again. We were perfect together. I did everything for her. I worshiped the ground she walked on, and all she did was walk all over me. I had to read text messages to find out how she really felt. She was the best thing to happen to me until she became the worst. It's not my fault, Ezra. She brought it on herself."

He processes that and then says, "And the next one? Same thing? You keep thinking you found *the one* but they treat you like shit?"

"Women are strange fucking creatures, man," I say with

a laugh. "I don't know that they know what they want half the time. You get the ones saying they want a nice guy, and hey, I'm fucking nice. I'm here, taking your dog out to take a shit because you're too sick to do it. I'm bringing you food and medicine while you're curled up in bed. I remember your favorite book and find you a special edition. I don't forget your favorite movie, and make sure it's on when you come over. I put gas in your car before you have to go to work the next day, because I know you're too fucking lazy to do it yourself. I do those things, but it's too much. I'm too nice. Too considerate. So what? You want the bad boy, right? The guy who barely acknowledges you. The one who uses you. Guess what happens when I treat them like a fucking sex toy? Oh, I'm a walking red flag, but these chicks fuck the bad boy when they have the nice guy. How am I supposed to keep up?"

My chest heaves as I finish talking, my teeth clenched and anger at a tipping point. Ezra's face remains impassive, unaffected by my roller coaster of emotions.

I force a laugh and shrug. "So, yeah. What're you gonna do?"

"And men? You don't do this with them?"

"It's different than when I'm with women. I want to be there for a woman. I want to step up and be the protector and caretaker, as long as they can fucking deal with the way I do it, and don't, you know, talk shit about me or cheat on me." I shake my head as I blow out a frustrated breath. "With men, I want the opposite, but most men don't know how to take care of anybody. Selfish, oblivious, and some-times just plain stupid." I pause and notice the way he's looking at me. "Not me, of course," I say with a twitch of my lips. "I'm not those things, Ezra."

He lifts his chin, but I can see the thoughts behind his

eyes. I've lifted the veil, and he's finally seeing a glimpse at who I am. He thinks he knows me now. He doesn't. Not truly, but do we ever really know anyone? Couples married for fifteen years have secrets. They have parts of them the other person doesn't know about. They have desires and fantasies, hopes and dreams, frustrations and resentment, and they don't reveal them. Only we know who we truly are at our core. Only we know what we're capable of and what we want.

"If you want two completely different things from different people, how will you ever be happy?" he asks. "Let's say you find a woman who lets you do all the things you want to do. She isn't bothered by you joining her on every outing she has, she's just as into you as you're into her. She loves you. She doesn't want anybody else."

"Uh-huh," I say, waiting for the rest.

"Well, first of all, I think you'd get bored, but you also want someone to take care of you. You want the same attention you give a woman, but you don't want it from a woman, do you?"

My face morphs before I even realize it. "No, I don't want a woman to possess me."

"Do you want a man to possess you? And if you find one who can, what about the compulsion to obsess over women?"

"It's not *obsession*," I say with a bite. I take a breath and drop my head back. "Guess I need one of each."

I hear him sigh, and when I lift my head, I find him leaning back. "You're exhausting."

"Yes, I'm quite the handful. That's why I have the problems I have."

"You'll never be satisfied."

"Will you? Tell me you don't miss it. The thrill. The rush of adrenaline. I know you want to do it again."

He ignores me. "I get why you snapped. The cheating. The lies. Most people want to kill the person who cheats on them, but usually, they have a stronger grip on—"

"Sanity?"

"I was gonna say morals, but okay. Sanity works too. But why? Why are you like that? Your parents?"

I stand up and walk to the kitchen. "That's another question for another day, but feel free to tell me what made you snap. Obviously it was your parents, but what did they do?"

He follows me. "Perhaps another day for that, too."

I pour us both two fingers worth of whiskey. "So, there will be another day," I say, passing him the glass. "Not gonna try to off me?"

"Are you planning on killing me? Or is that just reserved for women?"

I grin and take a sip. "I don't plan these things. Not really."

"So, then maybe I should take care of you right now. I could live in peace without the worry that you'll run your mouth or decide to try to kill me one day."

"I wouldn't kill you, Ezra."

"You *couldn't* kill me, Kaspian."

I bite my bottom lip before a smile takes over. "Don't underestimate me."

"Don't play with me."

"Like this?" I say, chancing a step in his direction as I slide my fingers into his waistband again.

His hand is around my throat in an instant. "If you even think about saying anything to anyone, I will end you before you even realize I'm a threat."

64

"You're always a threat."

"Don't forget it." He eases his grip but keeps his hand in place. It's probably because he just likes touching me, but I don't mind it.

"We could work together."

"What we do is different, and I don't work well with others."

My fingers unsnap the button before dragging his zipper down. "We're similar, you and me. It could be fun."

"I don't have a reason to anymore." He struggles to get the sentence out, long pauses between the words.

"Oh, you don't think I believe that, do you? Maybe you had a reason to kill the first two. Definitely the two who raped your friend, but what about the others? Were there reasons? Or did you simply have a need? An urge?"

I start to tug his pants and underwear down, and he keeps watching me.

"I told you. I don't want to have to worry about moving again. I'm fine with the way things are now."

"Are you?" I question. "Really?"

He ignores me because he knows his answer would be a lie. "Now that you've gotten my attention, what're you planning on doing next? Find more girls to follow?"

My fingers wrap around his shaft. "Would that make you jealous?"

He moans as I drag my fist down to his crown. "No. There's nothing between us."

My nostrils flare when I look at him. "I wouldn't say that."

His hand moves from my throat to my hair, yanking on the strands until my head is as far back as it can go. "You want me now, huh? That's what this is? You've used the girls, you've killed them, and it's my turn, right? You want me to take care of you? I'm supposed to fawn over you, care where you are and who you're with? You want me to be the daddy you likely didn't have? Is that it?"

I suck in deep breath through my nostrils, rage running through my veins as I clench my jaw. "Don't. Do not mention him."

His lips curl up into a snarl. Hardly a smile, but he's amused. "Ah, I'm starting to understand. Daddy didn't give you what you needed."

"Shut up," I say, releasing my grip on his cock and trying to push away.

He tightens his hold on my hair assuring I can't go anywhere. He's got maybe fifteen pounds on me, and it's all muscle.

"Daddy didn't give you any attention, did he? He didn't care about you. Wasn't there for you. Maybe he didn't love you. Daddy ignored you, didn't he?" His tone is nothing but mocking hostility.

"Stop it. You don't know what you're saying."

His arm wraps around my back to keep me from fighting out of his grip, pinning my arms down in the process. He smashes me into him, his expression wicked. This isn't Ezra. It's Quintin.

"That's why you need a man to obsess over you. You want that father figure, right? I'm guessing dear old Dad didn't discipline you either. You seek it out in men. That's why you like them dominant."

"You couldn't be dominant if you tried," I sneer. "Mr. I-have-to-have-reasons. There's no fucking moral code to killing. You don't get to make up an excuse to justify why you did it. You did it because you fucking wanted to. If you can't admit that, then—"

I'm spinning. He doesn't let me finish my rant, because

he releases his hold on me just to swirl me around and bend me over the kitchen counter. His cock presses into my ass while his hand comes down on the side of my head, pressing my cheek to the cold granite.

"Shut the fuck up." His voice is like gravel—rough, and it sends a thrill up my spine. "You like commanding men? Then do what the fuck I say and stay there."

He walks around me, his hand moving to my back while he uses his other one to open up drawers.

"What are you looking for?"

"Shut up."

"A knife? You gonna kill me?"

A drawer slams shut, and when he has to lean over to open the next one, his hand on my back lifts slightly, so I take the opportunity and run.

My feet pound across the wooden floor, taking me to the back. The barn house is mostly open concept, the living room, dining room, and kitchen all laid out together without any walls, but there are parts that I closed off. My downstairs bedroom is one of them, so I run through the one doorway near the back and cut to the right. Before I can close the door completely, it swings open with ferocity, forcing me to jump back.

Ezra, no, Quintin, stands there like a predator.

I keep taking steps backward until I run into my bed. I decide to sit down on the edge because there's no way I'm getting past him.

He stalks forward, slow and methodical. "I thought you liked being told what to do," he says, reaching out to grab my jaw. "I'm telling you right now, do not fucking run from me. You understand?"

I nod, my heart racing.

He squeezes my cheeks, yanking upwards and forcing

me to my feet. "I'm not going to kill you, Kas. Not until I have *reason* to," he snarls. "Don't give me a reason, okay?"

I dip my chin in acknowledgment, but it's not enough. He arches a brow and waits.

"Okay."

"Why did you take me to a kink club tonight?" he asks, reaching behind him.

"I uh..."

"Don't lie."

"I hoped it would move things along for us."

"How so?"

"Exactly how it happened."

He thinks for a second. "You orchestrated me finding you with that man."

"If you showed even the slightest bit of jealousy, I knew you were interested."

His arm comes out from behind his back, and in it, a knife. "You play too many games, and you're untrustworthy."

I eye the weapon in his hand. "And you're trustworthy?"

"No. That's why this thing between us could never be anything. We probably aren't even suitable for friendship."

"But?"

"But." He brings the tip of the knife to the center of my button up, the blade pricking my skin. "I'm still intrigued."

"Intrigued by what?" I ask.

He slides the knife inside my shirt before slowly dragging it down, cutting the strings from the buttons and allowing it to open up.

"You. I don't know nearly enough yet, and even though every instinct in me is saying I should stay away from you, I find myself interested in the challenge of dealing with you."

My lips curl into a crooked smirk. "Romantic."

His face goes blank and he gestures to the bed with the knife. "Lay down."

I'm quick to listen, discarding my ruined shirt in the process. When I'm settled on my back, head resting between the two pillows on my queen-size bed, he makes his way over.

"Arms up." From his back pocket, he removes two of the large zip ties I had in my kitchen drawer.

"Are you kidding?"

"No."

I lift my arms to the brass bars at the headboard, studying him as he secures my wrists. "I don't feel very safe. You could kill me pretty easily."

"I could kill you pretty easily even if you weren't tied to the bed."

"I know you don't have any experience with men, but I promise I could make you feel really good if I had use of my hands."

"I don't need your hands," he says, dropping the knife to the mattress before kicking off his shoes and removing his pants. "And you don't know about my experience with anything."

"Well, do you realize that to fuck me, there would need to be some sort of preparation?"

He smiles in a way that shows no humor. "Maybe you don't realize what's gonna happen here."

My heart leaps into my throat. I've always been excited by fear. I live for it. The thought of getting caught. The act of doing something wrong. But being vulnerable like this really ratchets the fear up to another level. I know I can't trust him, but there's part of me that believes he won't kill me. Not now. Not yet.

I've ensnared him. He doesn't know that everything I've

69

done was for him. Every move I've made was just a step in his direction. I don't mind playing a long game. I've got him now, though, and I won't lose him so easily. Whatever he wants to do, I'll allow, because I know I'm in charge, even when he thinks he is. There's still something I need to know, and he won't open up willingly. And there's still a decision I need to make, but in the meantime, I don't mind having a little fun.

You can sleep with people you hardly know, people you hate. Hell, even people you want to kill. Sex is nothing but physical pleasure. You don't need to be in love to do it.

He drops his underwear and climbs onto the bed, straddling my legs. I lick my lips as I take in the sight of him. Good god.

The intensity of his gaze as his eyes rake over me makes heat bloom in my chest. I focus on the set of his mouth, surrounded by his short-trimmed beard and mustache, and wonder if he tastes like the darkness that lives in his eyes.

His bronze body is flawless—the opposite of mine. He holds no tattoos, and besides the scar on his neck, he doesn't seem to have ever been injured. My skin, while having some color, is still paler than his, and decorated in ink and healed scars. I'm lean with some toned muscle, but he's cut. My eyes track the veins protruding in his biceps, traveling lower to his forearm where they sprawl out like vines.

I watch him work as he undoes my black slacks, pulling them past my ass, followed by my boxer-briefs. My cock springs free, slapping against my stomach with a smack.

Ezra reaches for his erection, stroking it as he stares at my dick. He doesn't say anything, but eventually, he reaches out and runs his other palm up my shaft.

"Shit," I cry, wanting more.

He leans over me, bracing himself on his forearms as his face moves closer to mine. The idea that he'd kiss me is fleeting. His mouth hovers near my ear, his hips rocking slowly, grinding his cock against mine. I yank on the restraints, wanting nothing more than to touch him.

"I'm going to use you, and there's nothing you can do about it."

The hair on my arms stand up as goosebumps travel the length of them.

He sits back up, bringing our cocks together in his hand as he strokes. I bite down on my lip, my chest rising and falling with deep breaths.

"Why did you bring me to that club? The real reason."

I groan as his hand moves up and down both our erections. "I told you."

"I said the real reason." He lets go of my dick and continues to stroke only himself.

"Because I wanted you. My," I pause, trying to find the best word, "fascination with you was at a boiling point. I thought I would be okay with just being friends, but you're like a magnet, and I'm iron. When I get too close, you pull me in, even if you don't mean to. It's hard to fight the attraction. I needed to be there with you, surrounded by people having sex, hoping it would give you a jumpstart to admitting you wanted me."

"Wanted," he says simply. "You said you *wanted* me."

"I still do."

"Why?"

His strokes are languid. He's not trying to get off, only making sure he stays hard.

"I like the way you look."

With a swift movement, he grabs the knife and slams it onto my sternum, lying flat.

"I don't like being lied to."

My stomach quivers and I shake my head. "I like the darkness in you. Makes me feel normal."

He takes a second to mull over my words and then his fingers wrap around the handle of the knife and he carefully drags the tip of the blade down the middle of my chest before bringing it to my heart.

He doesn't look at me, he just watches the knife. My breaths are ragged, fear and excitement mixing together.

"I went a long time trying to be normal. Society's version of normal, anyway. I thought I was content, even though the thoughts and urges never really went away. I was better at ignoring them, but by suppressing those needs, I changed a lot about who I am." He places the sharp edge against my skin, between my fourth and fifth ribs. His body vibrates with energy. He wants to do it again. "I miss the warmth of the blood on my fingers. The way life drains from their eyes as blood seeps from their bodies." He inhales deeply through his nose, his eyes finally landing on mine. "I thought I could be done, until you."

"What do you mean?" I ask in a quiet voice.

"When I suspected you were doing something to these women, I wanted to know more about you. I hoped to be able to catch you. To watch. I thought it would help to live vicariously. I'm not so sure anymore."

His grip tightens on the handle before he lifts it from my flesh.

"Do it," I say, telling myself it's bravery and not stupidity.

"What?" His brows furrow deeply, his face hard.

"Cut me. Don't kill me. Feel the blood between your fingers again."

His eyes show confusion, but it's quickly replaced by

72

exhilaration. Once again, his body trembles. The excitement is too much to contain.

"You don't know what you're asking."

"I'm giving you what you want."

"You're playing with your life. Who's to say I'll be able to control myself?"

I force a grin that I hope is as carefree as I want it to be. "If you kill me, you won't be able to do this again. If you keep me alive, we can have this forever."

His eyes narrow when I say the word *forever*. It was too much. Before I can backtrack, the blade penetrates my skin.

"Ah fuck," I hiss, looking down to see a droplet of blood emerge from the cut. Then another one, and another.

He drags the blade down in a curve, leaving a crescent moon shape in my flesh. He's not forcing the blade too deep into my body, but he's cutting deeply enough to produce a good amount of blood.

"Fuck," I curse, the burn turning into a throb.

Silently, he cuts the mirror image of the crescent moon, creating a circle on my left pec. The tip goes a little deeper at the base of his work, and I bite down on my bottom lip so hard that I draw blood.

He drops the knife and his fingers reach for the wound. Carefully, as if he doesn't want to disturb the pool of crimson, his fingertips slide into the liquid. His chest expands with a deep breath, and then he pushes down, causing more blood to surface. His hand smears the deep red color over my pec, coating his fingers. He inhales deeply, closing his eyes and dropping his head back as he relishes this moment.

His eyes finally find mine, like he's realizing I'm here for the first time. I lick my bottom lip, tasting blood, and his nostrils flare.

He takes his dick in his hand and starts stroking. My cock comes back to life as I watch him, his skin flushed, dick hard and painted with my blood. With his left hand, he touches me, his thumb swiping at the pre-cum dripping from my crown. From there, his fingers find my lip and swipe at the blood. He mixes them together, his eyes transfixed on the liquid between his fingertips. His other hand moves faster on his dick.

We're nothing but heavy breaths and grunts. His eyes bounce between his own dick, to mine, to the blood on my chest.

"Fuck," he groans, releasing my cock as an orgasm overtakes him.

When he roars, his cum shoots out in white ribbons, landing on my dick and lower stomach. I watch patiently as his body rocks with aftershocks, his back hunched as he squeezes out every drop of his cum onto my skin.

My dick throbs with need, pain already forgotten.

"Ez," I rasp in a husky tone. "Please." I jerk on my restraints as I look at him.

He stands and grabs my ruined shirt from the floor to wipe his dick before he starts to get dressed. This has got to be a cruel joke.

"What're you doing?" I ask, struggling to keep the alarm from my tone.

Once his pants are fastened and his shoes are on his feet, he comes forward. "Kaspian, you have to know this won't work."

"What the fuck are you talking about?" I say, jerking my arms and trying to sit up.

"I'll admit you aroused my curiosity, but I'm sure this won't end well."

"You call this ending well?" I snap.

"We're both alive," he says with a shrug.

"Are you afraid? Is that it? You're afraid that by being around me you won't be able to control yourself? I let you cut me, Ezra. I can give you what you want while also allowing you to be a hundred percent yourself. You don't have to lie to me. You don't have to pretend."

"And that's why it's dangerous. I'm only free because I've never told anyone anything, but now you're here and trying to get me to do what will only get me caught and locked up. Plus, I know you're still lying to me. I don't trust you. And you have your own fucked up hobbies. You want a happily ever after? You want us to leave the house, have me go kill someone while you stalk someone else, then we come back for dinner like that's fucking normal?"

"There is no normal!" I shout. "We could do whatever the fuck we want."

He leans down, his hand grabbing my face. "I'm doing what I want. Don't ruin it. Don't give me a reason to end you, Kas. I know you can be obsessive, but aim that shit somewhere else, okay?"

Fury boils beneath the surface of my skin. He doesn't even know what he's talking about. Foolish.

Grabbing for the knife, he cuts the zip tie from my left hand before placing the knife just out of reach on the nightstand.

"You'll get to it eventually and be able to cut the other one off. I don't trust that you won't chase me down. You understand."

"You're not thinking straight. You don't know what we could have."

"There isn't a *we*, Kaspian. There isn't a *forever* either."

He walks out of the room, my blood staining his hand, his cum coating my skin, and he thinks there isn't an us.

75

EZRA

TEN

Two weeks go by without seeing Kas. Two weeks and three days, to be exact. It's too long to be normal. You can't avoid people here. After the first handful of days, I briefly worried he was still tied to his bed, unable to get free. He's smart though. Definitely capable of getting out of harder traps. The knife was nearby. Even with one hand tied to the bed, he'd be able to get up and reach it.

I couldn't cut him loose completely. Without a car, I had a long trek to the highway where I eventually met up with an Uber driver. I didn't want to risk him catching up.

Now, however, I wonder what he's up to. Though most of me doesn't believe he'll tell anyone what he knows about me, there will always be a small concern that he will, and that concern will continue to grow unless I handle him.

I'll admit I underestimated him. He was aware of me watching him from the beginning. Had even been watching me first. He had done research and found out who I used to be. Sort of impressive, but mostly frustrating. I can't slip back. I don't want to be Quintin.

Ezra Hamilton is far different from Quintin Black.

Kaspian makes it too easy to be Quintin. His permission. Encouragement. It's tempting to run with it, but I can't. Not unless...

No! I can't.

You see, Quintin killed his parents. And if someone can kill their own parents, then there isn't much hope for anyone else. Who's safe if the people who brought him into the world weren't?

After them, I knew I needed a cover. I had to create a serial killer. I had to become one in order to be safe. The cops were suspicious. I was a young college kid home for the summer. I didn't have a motive, but my alibi was shaky. I was out with a girl that night. She told them we had been drinking and she didn't remember much after going to bed. I insisted I was in her bed all night, but one of the cops looked at me like he saw who I was. He didn't believe it, but there wasn't proof either way.

My third kill was a few weeks later, because I needed them to look elsewhere. I spent the night with another woman, and she was my alibi. She never knew I slipped out into the night when she fell asleep. Alcohol wasn't the reason that time. I didn't want to risk that being a pattern. However, she had a slight allergy to cats, and I had been sure to visit my friend's house, which was filled with them, before I went to hers. They were all over me, rubbing their bodies against my legs, climbing into my lap as I sat on the couch. Their fur was on every inch of my clothing. She wasn't going to die, but she had enough of a reaction that she became itchy and her nose ran, and she needed to take some medicine. Medication that would make her sleepy.

The fourth was a little over a month later, and the news started running with the idea of a potential serial killer in the Seattle area.

I could've stopped then. I did. For a while.

Then those two assholes raped and beat Leslie and hardly got a slap on the wrist. The serial killer had to strike again.

It'd be a lie to say I didn't enjoy it. There's an art to it. You can't do it out in the open. You can't be angry and sloppy. You have to be methodical. You have to have a plan. There's even a thrill in the buildup to the big moment.

The times after then were sporadic. It's dangerous, after all. I did what I could; it was never anybody that would be missed. Nobody with a family that would report them missing. Some I was able to dispose of, some were found and added to the tally of the Heart Stopper.

The last one was right before I moved here. I thought he was just another addict on a corner street, begging for dope from anyone who walked by. When I approached him, asking if he was interested in a score, I got him to follow me to my workstation. He probably thought it was another drug den, but it was the perfect spot to do what I do. Not many people went on that side of town, nor strayed that far from the main road. It was a dilapidated house, its image discouraging people from exploring it. There wasn't any electricity, and a lot of the windows were busted in. I used wood to cover them up. It's not like I needed an audience anyway.

He followed me there, believing that's where the drugs were, instead it's where he met his fate. After untying him, I began to clean up. I removed his wallet and any personal effects, and low and behold, he was a fucking undercover cop.

Killing a junkie is one thing. Murdering a cop is a whole nother. Cops don't give a shit about who they consider lowlifes. They come across a dead addict? They'll hardly look into it. They'll say they deserved to die. You kill a cop though? You'll have the entire brotherhood of blue on your back.

I'll admit, it shook me up. They'd come looking for him. They'd know where he was working. He would have to check in at some point. It was my biggest mistake. I wasn't aware there was some sort of operation in the area. Someone was selling laced heroin that was killing its users, and the cops were hoping to catch them.

I didn't have time to dismember him or wrap him up. I couldn't chance hauling away his body in case anyone saw. I had to leave him there, thereby giving up my workplace. I did the best cleanup job you could do in a house like that, getting rid of any evidence that I may have had there. But before I walked away for the last time, I had to ruin my work. He had been stabbed just between his ribs. Like the others. I couldn't leave him that way. I didn't want a cop to be added to the list of victims for the Heart Stopper. I had to make it a little sloppier.

The only good thing about the location is that the cops would take one look and assume it was where drug addicts and homeless people went. It might've been at one point. When I found it, the only changes I made were to board up the windows and put locks on the doors. Nobody would ever be able to get in there while I was. I was sure to remove the hardware I installed before I left.

I fled shortly after. His death was on the news constantly. Most assumed an addict killed him. Some thought it was a drug dealer who found out he was a cop. Even though nobody had any reason to link it to the Heart Stopper, or to Quintin Black, I couldn't stick around.

So, here I am, a Soledad Square resident after attempting to live in New Mexico for a brief time. There, in the Land of Enchantment, a new killer emerged. I didn't want to be the Heart Stopper anymore. I couldn't resurrect him and have it all over the news. The few people in New Mexico were killed in different ways, as to not create a pattern. None of it was as satisfying though. Once I lost the thrill, I decided to move on, and that's how I ended up here, trying to be a normal citizen. I can't kill people the way I want to. Not without bringing heat to my back, and I don't want to do it any other way.

Nobody knows about my stint in the southwest region of the United States. Not even Kaspian with all his research and background checks. There's no way that was traceable.

Kaspian.

Where the fuck is he and what is he up to? I know I shouldn't care. He's doing what I told him to do, but I find his acquiescence strange.

"Hey, Ezra," Willow chirps as I walk into work.

"Hey, Will," I reply with a nod.

She groans. "Could you at least call me Low or something? Will is too masculine, and I'm dainty," she says with a flirty grin.

I quickly notice her tight jeans and snug sweater, showcasing the curves of her hips and the swell of her breasts. "Got it."

Willow smiles. "Got any plans this weekend? Haven't seen you at The Hideout lately."

I haven't been since that time with Kaspian.

"No, not really."

"It's Halloween," she says, as if that's reason enough to go out.

"The holiday where kids ask for candy?" I muse.

She rolls her eyes. "The holiday where adults can dress up and get drunk." She walks away from the water cooler with a small cup and drops into her seat behind the desk. "There's a bar crawl this weekend. Between Park Avenue and Aurora Road there's like eight different bars and pubs, and everyone is gonna dress up and visit all of them. It'll be fun. You should come."

I make a face. "I don't know."'

"Oh, come on. Please," she says with a pout, her clasped hands resting under her chin. "You can leave after the first bar if you're not having fun."

She's cute and sweet, and I've declined several other invites, so I agree.

"Fine. But I'm not dressing up."

"What? You have to!"

She goes on for a while about why I need to dress up, and even attempts to give me simple ideas. We end up talking for a while, and I find out more about her in thirty minutes than I have in the last year and a half that I've been working here. Guess it's safe to say I've been pretty closed off.

"Let me give you my number," she says. "You can text me on Friday night and I'll tell you where to meet me." I hand her my phone and watch as her manicured nails tap on my screen. The swoosh sound of a text being sent follows. "I texted myself, so now I have your number, too."

She blushes slightly when she returns the phone. I smile at her and slip it into my pocket.

"Guess I should get to work," I tell her.

"Guess so."

I've always thought I couldn't have a normal dating life. Everyone I've slept with has been temporary. One night, or sometimes three. But maybe if I gave Willow a chance we could have something longer than that. She'll never know who I really am. She won't be able to meet Quintin. She'll never let me cut her while I stroke my cock. She won't accept that dark part of me, but maybe this is another step I need to take in order to be normal. There's a chance that being with her, and all the light she brings into a room, will make me want to be a better person rather than slip into old ways.

Maybe, but I won't hold my breath.

CHAPTER
ELEVEN

I get a text from Willow at six o'clock, giving me an address and the command to be in costume. Behind that, a very serious looking emoji.

At five-fifty-nine, I knock on the door of the duplex. When the door swings open, I can hardly keep my jaw from dropping.

Willow has always been a cute, sweet girl. Tonight, Willow is a fucking goddess. She's wearing a tight, black bodysuit, fishnet stockings, black, thigh-high boots, and a black and white spotted cape. Long, red gloves cover her arms to the elbows, leaving the rest bare. A black and white wig replaces her usual honey-brown hair, and bright red lipstick paints her pouty mouth.

"You're the sexiest Cruella I've ever seen," I say.

She smiles, her cheeks turning pink. "Thank you. Come inside real quick."

I follow her into the cozy apartment, all of the lights off except the one in the kitchen, which is where she leads me. Spinning around, she eyes me up and down.

"Okay, I'm trying to guess what this could possibly be, but I'm getting nothing. You didn't take any of my ideas."

"I'm Wolverine."

She chokes out a laugh. "You are not."

"I am. Look, a white tank top. Jeans."

Willow sputters out another laugh. "Stop it. You're not serious. You don't even have the claw things, or the hair-style. Or sideburns!" She cracks up some more.

I chuckle along with her. "It's the best I could do on short notice."

She waves her hand in the air. "No, we can do better." Turning around, she rifles through some drawers and tosses items on the counter.

I can't help but check out her long legs and plump ass cheeks that stick outside the edge of her bodysuit.

"The tank top I like," she says, spinning back around and studying my arms. "But let's add to it. You don't care if this gets ruined, do you?"

"No, it's fine."

She holds up a red bottle. "Blood. Well, fake blood. Take off your shirt so I can make some adjustments."

I pull the white material over my head and hand it to her. Her hazel eyes drink me in before she snaps out of her daze and gives me a shy grin. "Thanks."

I watch over her shoulder as she cuts a tear into the front of my shirt and uses a variety of tactics to cover the material with fake blood.

By the time she's done, it has a couple bloodied hand-prints, some darker drops and streaks, along with a spatter.

She washes her hands and puts her gloves back on before reaching for the cigarette holder on the counter. "Come on, darling. Let's let that dry," she says in her best Cruella voice before sashaying into the living room.

"Nice work."

She laughs. "It's Halloween. You can put blood on anything and make it work. You could either be a victim or a killer." She freezes. "Wait! Come back in here."

She takes hold of my wrist and brings me back to the kitchen. After grabbing the small spray bottle she used earlier, that's mixed with paint and water, she turns to face me.

"Can I?" Her eyes move to my torso as she holds up the bottle. "You can't just have a bloody shirt. If you killed someone, you'd have blood on your skin too, right?"

I stare into her eyes and shrug. "I guess."

She sprays the liquid on my chest, the cold making me twitch.

"Sorry," she says with a giggle before spraying my arms and my neck. "There. Don't worry. It'll be easy to come off."

"Easier than real blood, probably."

She laughs. "Yeah, probably. Let me run to my room real quick. I think I have something."

As she wanders through the doorway in the living room, I take a few moments to look around. She has picture frames everywhere, and my eyes dance over them, not getting too close. I don't want her to think I'm snooping. Her smiling face is in most of them, joined by an older couple, maybe parents, and an even older couple, probably grandparents. Some younger kids join her in others, two dogs, and girls her age. She's clearly got a good amount of friends and family, and more than that, they all seem to like each other.

"I found this in my closet from last year," she says, appearing behind me holding a knife.

"Oh."

She slices it through the air. "Yeah, I was a female

87

Chucky last Halloween."

"Probably the best looking Chucky there's ever been."

Her lips curl into a smile. "It's just a small plastic knife. Fake blood on it, but it completes your outfit."

I take it and slip into my belt loop. "Thanks."

She checks me out, her gaze flickering down my arms and across my chest and abs before she meets my eyes again. With a lift of her brow, she gives a little shrug, as if to say she's not embarrassed to have been caught.

"Guess we should start our night," she states, strutting to the kitchen once more. "But let's take a shot first." While she's pouring us each a shot of tequila, I pick up the shirt and carefully pull it over my head. She hands me a glass and clinks hers against mine. "To monsters and ghosts, and the things that frighten us most."

I smirk at her toast and swallow down the liquor, a trail of fire burning my throat.

Her apartment is a block away from Park Avenue, so we walk over and slip inside the first bar on the map. A literal map of a three-block radius that tells us which bars are participating. No wonder it starts so early.

Inside the Royal Lion, we meet up with a few of her friends and squeeze through the costumed people to get a drink.

Willow never leaves my side, making sure to introduce me to everyone and keep me in the conversation so I won't feel left out. I think it's because she's trying to make sure I don't decide to leave after this, but it could also just be because she's a decent person.

I remember a couple of her friends' names—Samantha and Cora, and a boyfriend of somebody's, whose name is BJ. A couple other women whose names I've already forgotten hang around us as well, and two other guys who I think Willow said went to school with her, but I don't recall their names either. Honestly, I'm bad at names, but good with faces.

Conversation flows, transitioning from their friend Emerson, who had a family emergency come up and had to leave, to a hot guy that works out at the only gym in town, to drama about an ex, and everything in between.

Willow leans over to fill me in as it goes. *Friend from middle school. I don't go to the gym, so I don't know who they're talking about. Cora's ex cheated on her with a mutual friend.*

It isn't until we're at the second bar that one of the guys in our group starts talking to me. I believe his name is Jason. Or maybe I made that up because he's dressed as Jason.

"You didn't grow up here, did you?"

"No. I'm guessing you did."

He grins. "Yeah. It's one of those places. You get stuck here. What made you choose this town?"

I shrug. "Seemed nice and quiet. Safe."

He nods, taking a sip from his beer. "Yeah, it's usually that. There's a few things here and there."

"Oh yeah?" I ask, thinking about Kaspian and his victims. I wonder if he's talking about missing women.

"Yeah. Anyway, so are you and Willow dating?" he says, moving on fast.

"No. We work together."

He gives me a sly grin, like he doesn't believe me. "I see."

I shake my head. "It's not like that."

"Okay," he says with a smile, and in a tone that lets me know he isn't buying it.

Just then, Willow runs up and grabs my arm. "Ezra, come here. You have to see this costume."

Jason winks at me, smiling like an idiot.

I stick around for the third and fourth bars, and by then, nearly everyone in the group is fairly tipsy. Willow promises we're going to stop and get food before heading to the next one. Alcohol makes these people happier. That isn't always the case, but it's been a fun night, and I've gotten to know a few of Willow's friends enough to know I don't hate them. Jason, which is his real name, has been hanging out with me a lot, considering he's not too fond of BJ. Willow dances with her friends while me and Jason hang out near the bar. When he excuses himself to take a piss, I use the break to go outside and smoke.

I'm sure to take several steps away from the door before I pull out my steel cigarette case and pop one into my mouth. Leaning against the corner of the building, I get a view of the intersecting streets and watch a couple clowns run up and scare the shit out of some girls dressed as sexy versions of Disney princesses.

"Halloween allows you to dress up as your real self without anyone being the wiser."

I blow out the smoke and turn my head to my right to find Kaspian at my side, a small grin on his lips. He's dressed in his normal clothes with a mask pushed up to the top of his head.

"Should've dressed as Michael Myers," I say. "Fits you."

"Too on the nose," he replies, coming around to stand directly in front of me. "I see you didn't care about that. It's funny," he says, stoned faced. "Did you get turned on when you covered yourself in fake blood?"

"It wasn't my idea, and I didn't do this," I reply, gesturing to my shirt before taking another drag.

"No? Whose idea was it?" he asks, head tilted.

I don't want to tell him about Willow. He can't be

trusted.

"Where did you disappear to?" I ask instead, regretting it.

His lips draw up at the corners. "Noticed me missing, huh? I thought that's what you wanted."

"It is. Yet, here you are."

"Oh, Ez. You missed me," he croons. "Admit it. You thought about me several times."

I take a drag and blow the smoke into his face. "Not really."

His hand reaches up and gently touches his chest. "I've thought about you. Hard not to with the souvenir you left me."

My eyes flicker to the area he's touching and then to his eyes. Memories flash in my mind. "Hmm."

"Mm." He moans lightly, dropping his hand and stepping forward to rest against the wall next to me. "I got you something."

My phone buzzes in my pocket, so I pull it out and look at the screen. It's a message from Willow asking where I went.

Kaspian shifts, pressing his shoulder to the brick while he stares at me. I lift my head and face him, seeing the anger in his eyes.

"Who's Will?"

"Why do you care?"

"Why wouldn't I?"

I turn so he can't see the screen and type out a response before I slip the phone back in my pocket. "You're not playing the jealous lover, are you? I haven't even fucked you."

His dark eyes narrow before he exhales, his face returning to nonchalance. "You can do whatever you want,

91

Ezra, but you'll always know that you can only ever be Quintin with me. And that's what you really want."

"You don't know me as well as you think you do. I don't want to be Quintin ever again, and I guarantee you don't want me to be either."

He exaggerates a shiver. "Mm. Dangerous. You have to know I like that."

I shake my head before I take a final drag. Kaspian takes the cigarette from my hand, his fingers brushing against mine. His eyes remain locked on my face as he brings the butt to his lips, sucking in the nicotine.

"That'll kill you," I tell him.

As he blows out the smoke, he says, "I just want a taste of your lips, even if I have to risk dying to get it."

He drops the butt and puts it out with the toe of his boot, crowding my space as he steps forward. His hand grazes my cock as he leans in close to my ear.

"Let me know when you're done with Will, then we can have some real fun. My gift to you is waiting, and it won't last long."

He backs up, his eyes focused on mine as he drags his thumb over his lip. He's the embodiment of dark and dangerous, seductively so. He knows exactly what to do—and how—to get my attention.

After turning and taking a few steps away from me, he slips his mask in place.

"Kaspian."

He turns around to reveal a shattered doll mask with black eyes and a slash through the mouth from ear to ear. "Yes?"

"What did you do?"

Even though I can't see his expression under the mask, I can visualize the smug, crooked grin he's giving me.

TWELVE

"Everything okay?" Willow asks when I return to the bar.

"Yeah. Went for a smoke break and ran into a friend."

"Okay, cool. We're getting ready to head to the next bar."

Our group of about eight walks to the end of Park Avenue and turn in the direction Kaspian went. At the next street, we go left and find ourselves in a sports bar. Decorations hang from the ceiling and are plastered on the walls. People pose for photos they'll be sure to have up on Instagram tomorrow morning, and I find my normal citizen mask begin to slip.

This isn't me. Not at my core. I've been pretty good at being charming enough to be liked but make it a point to not be too talkative. Being too loquacious can often annoy people, plus I'd be spewing mostly lies if I had to be the life of the party. I don't want that much attention.

It's hard to find the right balance.

I'm antisocial. I don't like crowds, clubs, parties, or

people in general. I've had my fill for the night, and I'm sure I've done a good enough job that everybody who's seen me will believe I had a good time. The truth is, I'm not stimulated by bar hopping. I find it boring, and Kaspian's mysterious gift calls to me.

Jason nudges my arm as I plan my escape. "I'm better than BJ, right?" He's nearly drunk, staring at Samantha and BJ as they dance.

"Definitely got the better name," I say. We laugh together.

"I don't know what she sees in him. If only she knew what I do."

Through the night, I've come to find out that Jason is in love with Samantha, but she doesn't see him in that light. BJ is an asshole with some secrets.

"Tell her," I say with a shrug.

"She'd hate me."

"Figure out how to tell her anonymously."

His brows furrow as he mulls it over. "Maybe." He starts nodding his head. "Yeah, that could work. Thanks, man."

I smile at him. Maybe it's not normal to recommend sabotaging someone's relationship for your own benefit, but hey, it's not like I told him to kill BJ.

"Hey, let's do some shots," I say with a wide grin that I don't mean. "I'll grab them."

"Ezra's getting shots," Jason announces to the group. Everyone cheers.

When I'm back with a tray of liquor, I happily pass them out to everyone, smiling and laughing, and fitting in with everyone else. "To new friends!" I say, giving Willow a coy smile. She beams back at me and we down our drinks.

I let a good fifteen minutes go by and make sure I wait until I'm near everyone in the group before I pull out my phone and pretend to answer a call. Because it's so loud, I have to go outside to hear, so they understand.

I take a deep breath when I'm out in the cool air and drop my head against the wall. My phone dings in my hand.

802-555-9066: *Tick Tock*

I DON'T HAVE to question who it is, but I still have an inquiry.

ME: *How did you get my number?*

As I WAIT for his reply, Jason bursts through the door. "Hey, man. Fucking Cora is throwing up in the bathroom, so like the good guy that I am, I'm gonna make sure she gets home. Nobody else wants their night to end. Think Samantha will notice?"

I want to say probably not, but I do what I do and lie. "Yeah, man. She better. You're the only one who offered to help her friend."

He smiles and nods like he's excited that I agree. "Everything okay with you?" he says gesturing to the phone.

I look down and another message appears.

802-555-9066: *Tell Will to get lost before I make sure he's never found.*
    Me: *Fucking stalker.*

. . .

IT TAKES effort to not smile, but I look up and shake my head. "Family emergency. My mom is trying to reach me about my dad. He's been sick for a while. I should head home and call her back."

"Damn, that sucks. Sorry, man."

I squeeze the bridge of my nose and make a face. "Think Willow will be mad?"

"Nah." He shakes his head. "I'll explain. Go ahead and go. I'll talk to you later." He squeezes my shoulder, trying to give me some comfort. "I hope everything is okay."

I offer him a smile, mostly because I know Kaspian is watching. "Thanks. I appreciate it."

He disappears inside and I go back to my phone as I spin around and walk away.

802-555-9066: *His hand will go first.*

I LAUGH ALOUD, and it's the first genuine laugh I've had in a while. Kaspian's craziness is amusing.

ME: *Where are you?*

I TURN the corner and get almost all the way down Park Avenue without a response. I have to walk another block and a half before I get to Willow's street so I can retrieve my car.

"Here I am," Kaspian says, appearing at my side.

I try to hide my jolt as best I can. I didn't see him coming. "You're a crazy person, you know that?"

His smile is evil. "Yes."

I shake my head. "Where's my present?"

"Oh, so you want it?"

"Why must you play these games?" I say through an exhale.

"Did you get tired of Will? Decided I offered a little more excitement?"

"That wasn't Will, and he's straight, if you must know."

"Right. Seemed very flirty tonight. Lots of laughter, winking, touching." His jaw clenches as he stares at me.

"How long were you watching me tonight?"

His lips twist, fighting a grin, but he changes the subject as usual. "You giving me a ride tonight?"

"Where's your car?"

"That's not what I meant," he says, wiggling his brows as he bites his bottom lip through a smile. When I give him an apathetic look, he laughs. "You'll want to once you see what I have for you. You'll want to give me everything."

"I think you overestimate my desire for gifts."

"I think you underestimate my gift giving abilities." He goes quiet for a few seconds. "Plus, let's not pretend you don't want to fuck me."

I ignore that comment.

"So, your place?" I ask.

"Yep. Remember how to get there?"

"Yeah."

He goes to turn, but spots my car a few houses away, parked under a streetlight.

"That Jason's house? Or Will's?"

"Don't."

His eyes flicker to the duplex, and now I wonder if I put Willow in danger. I'm not exactly compassionate, but

Willow doesn't need to walk into her place and find a crazed Kaspian there.

I grab his chin roughly, forcing him to look at me. "It's not a man's place. You hear me? Do not give me a reason, Kaspian. I'm telling you."

Kas's face changes minutely. He likes when I touch him.

"A woman's then?" he asks, voice softer. When I don't answer right away, he continues. "Because I can deal with you being with a woman. They offer what I can't. But not a man, Ezra. I wouldn't take too well to that."

"We are not together, Kaspian."

He reaches down to rub my crotch. "I know, but we can still have fun. Let's go."

THIRTEEN

By the time I show up to Kaspian's house, he's already there, the lights inside shining through every window. His figure crosses in front of one of them before the front door opens. He leans against the door jamb, watching me with a cocksure grin.

I exit the car and stroll up to him.

"Welcome back," he says, barely containing his excitement.

"Shut up."

He snorts and backs up, letting me in before closing and locking the door. "Drink?"

"I'm good."

Kaspian picks up a mug from his end table and takes a sip. After replacing it, he says, "Well, follow me."

My heart thumps in my chest as he leads me to the back of his house. Not out of fear, but excitement, because if I know anything about Kaspian it's that he's got a twisted way of thinking. He was gone for two weeks and now he's back with a gift. I don't take him for a chocolate and teddy bear kind of guy, so if my gut is right, I think I know what I'll find.

Inside the laundry room there's another doorway. He bends down to lift up the door, revealing a hatch.

"What am I about to find, Kaspian?" I ask, breaking the silence.

"You want me to ruin the surprise?"

He turns and looks at me as he descends the steps. I follow him, my pulse spiking as we lower ourselves deeper into the darkness.

Kaspian's hand brushes against mine, and then he's gone, a light flickering to life to my right before a few more turn on. It's massive and somewhat jarring. Broken concrete makes up the floor, and beams and poles are everywhere. Looks like a good section is split into stalls.

"What the hell went on here?" I ask.

"Probably where they slaughtered the animals."

"Well, thank you for this beautiful gift."

He laughs and takes my hand. "Come on."

We walk to the end, approaching a section that's blocked by what looks like a newly erected wall. When Kaspian pulls me around the partition, he gestures with his other arm like he's presenting me with a brand-new car. Instead, I find a man tied to a concrete slab, eyes covered and mouth gagged. He's only wearing pants, and he's completely still.

"Who is this?"

Kaspian leans against the wall. "Your gift."

"I gathered," I say, walking toward the man. "Explain."

"I'm just trying to get you to understand that I get you. You don't have to be anybody but yourself with me. You want this. You crave this," he says, gesturing to the motionless figure. "I'm giving it to you, and I'm the only one who can."

I take a deep breath. "Don't act like this is completely selfless."

He smiles. "Of course it's not. I want you to appreciate what I've done for you. I want you to reward me."

I stare at him for several seconds. "Where did he come from?"

"Out of town. No connections."

"How'd you lure him here?"

"Well," he says with a head tilt. The man on the slab starts moving. Kaspian's eyes bounce between me and him. "You gonna do this? One way or another, we have to get rid of him. He's seen my face."

When the man hears our voices, he starts making noise and jerking against the ropes. Kaspian moves to a corner where there's a small toolbox. When he walks back toward me, he holds out his hand and shows me a thirteen-inch, black stiletto knife.

My eyes dart to his. He knew the right type of knife to get. "I can't. I can't bring him back," I say, alluding to Quintin.

He shakes his head. "He won't be found. There will be no way for anybody to pin this on you."

I reach out and take the knife, running my finger along the blade. My body trembles as Ezra disappears and Quintin emerges. I toss the knife in the air, watching it flip before it lands in my hand. I gaze at Kaspian, my lips pulling into a nefarious grin. His eyes light up.

Standing beside the man, I remove his blindfold. He squints before he notices Kaspian, and then his eyes go wide and he looks at me, moaning and murmuring behind his gag, pleading with me through his frightened eyes.

I bring the knife up and place it against the black material stretched tight across his face. "Shh."

He freezes, quieting only slightly.

Kaspian moves back, watching from a stool in the corner.

I cut the cloth, nicking his face in the process, then I remove the ball of material from his mouth and toss it aside.

"Please, man. Please. Oh god. Don't kill me. I don't know what I did."

He's frantic. Terrified. Desperate. Everything I love. It fills me with power.

"What did he do, Kaspian?" I ask, watching the man's face.

He tries to find him but can't move enough to get a good look. "I didn't do anything! I swear. He came on to me! I didn't touch him. I'm not a fucking fa—"

Before he can even finish producing the g on the word he was about to spew, I squeeze his cheeks together, halting his speech altogether.

"Don't do that," I say. "Don't succumb to hate."

My eyes travel to where Kaspian sits, transfixed. Almost amused.

"He wasn't so quick to hurl slurs when he had his hand down my pants," Kas replies, spinning a ring on his finger.

My grip tightens on the man's face as my jaw clenches. "Interesting."

The man tries shaking his head, attempting to speak again. His dirty blond hair sticks to his forehead with sweat, and his blue eyes peer up at me. I remove my hand. "You said don't succumb to hate, but what is this?" he cries.

"It's not hate. I don't feel passionately about your existence. I don't have an intense aversion to you."

"Then this makes no sense! He brought me here. He lied to me. Tricked me. Why?" he cries.

I lock eyes with Kas. "For me," I answer, receiving a smile.

"It wasn't a trick," Kaspian says. "He knew why he was coming with me. To fuck me. To suck my dick. To have his way with me."

He's spurring me on. I know he wants me to be jealous. I look down at the man who keeps fighting his restraints.

"You'll regret it. Don't do this for him. He's not even man enough to kill me himself. He's making you do the work for him. You'll have to live with this for the rest of your life."

Kaspian shakes his head, rolling his eyes.

My fingers land on his chest and I start counting. Kas leans forward.

"I don't live with regrets. Everything I've done, I've done because I wanted to."

I position the knife and shove it in at just the right angle. With an extra thrust, I push the blade in deeper and watch as his mouth parts, eyes bulging before I rip the knife out and blood begins to ooze out.

Placing the knife next to his body, I watch as life slowly drains away, the light in his eyes fading, his noises quieting.

Kaspian gets up and comes around to look as well.

"Welcome back, Quintin," he says with a tiny smirk.

With my bloodied hand, I reach out and grab his throat, walking him backward into the wall.

KASPIAN

CHAPTER
FOURTEEN

My head hits the wall before his hips are against mine. "You let him touch you."

"I didn't have a choice," I breathe, thrilled with his jealousy.

"What else did you two do?"

"Not much."

He undoes his pants with one hand while holding me in place with the other. "You found him for me."

Not a question, but I answer anyway. "Yes."

"While he was touching you, you thought about me, didn't you?"

He strokes himself between us.

"Yes."

"Touch me."

His cock is in my hand in the next second, and I stroke his thick length. He's rock hard and hot in my palm. He releases his hold on me, bracing himself on the wall on either side of my head, rolling his neck.

I slowly drop to my knees, forcing him back a step, and while looking into his eyes I take him into my mouth.

"Fuck," he hisses, fingers threading through my hair. It's the gentlest he's been. "Oh yeah."

I let his crown slide across my tongue, making its way to the back of my throat before I pull away and stroke.

"Jesus," he sighs, his grip tightening, pulling the strands taut.

My hands slide around his thighs, cupping his ass as I move my head back and forth until I allow him to slip from my mouth. My tongue glides across the underside of his shaft until I reach his balls.

He moans, staring down at me as I take them in my mouth one at a time.

His resolve snaps and he takes his dick in his hand and forces me back against the wall. His thumb slides into my mouth before he forces my lips apart, rubbing his pre-cum over my lips before forcefully thrusting inside.

"You don't know what you've done," he murmurs, fucking my mouth hard, his cock stretching my lips wide around him.

I groan around his width as he uses both hands to hold my head in place, ravaging my mouth, making me gag and drool.

"Fuck, your mouth feels so good." I moan, my cock throbbing behind my jeans. He pulls away suddenly and saliva drips down my chin. "Get up. Pants off."

I wipe my mouth and do as he says, desperate for more.

He strokes himself vigorously as he watches me. When I'm naked from the waist down, he grabs my hips and spins me around, bending me over the concrete slab. He shoves the man's legs over so I have room to rest my arms. What a romantic.

It's sick to do this near someone's dead body. I fucking love it.

His rough hand travels up my back, making me shiver. I feel him jerking off behind me, and then he kicks my legs apart wider. "Spread yourself for me," he demands, voice rough.

I reach behind me and do what he commanded, and before I know what's happening, I feel the warmth of his release on my ass. It drips between my cheeks.

"Oh fuck. Yes," he moans, dragging out the word.

His head smears the cum around my hole, and then his cock is replaced by his fingers. Two of them dip inside me.

"Oh god," I moan.

"God wouldn't dare step foot down here," he says, moving his fingers faster, pulling out only to swipe more of his cum and use it as lubrication.

"Please," I beg.

His chest touches my back as he leans over me, his lips touching my ear. "Have you been fucking anyone without a condom?"

I shake my head quickly. "Never."

"Until now."

His heat disappears as he moves back, and then his cock is pushing inside me.

"Shit," I roar, my hands flying to the concrete slab, gripping the edges. "Fuck."

"You can take it," he growls, pulling out slightly. He spits and then slides back in. "That's it. Mmm."

"Jesus," I cry. "Oh my god."

His hands squeeze my hips before one travels around to my cock. He strokes it a few times before bringing his hand to my lips. "Spit."

I do and he goes back to jerking me off and fucking me simultaneously. The burning pain morphs into pleasure as I begin to adjust to his size. My need to get off outweighs any of the pain that comes along with little prep. I've been dying to have him fuck me, and now it's happening, so I'm not about to complain.

"Fuck your fist," he says, moving one hand to my shoulder and the other to my hip, fucking me relentlessly.

My fist moves up and down my shaft as he grunts behind me.

"So tight. Fuck. So good." His words are short and simple, but I love that he's getting off to my body. I love that he loves the way I feel. "Come for me, Kaspian," he growls. "Show me just how much you love having me deep inside you."

I moan, my hand moving faster. "Fuck, Quin. Your dick feels so good. I don't ever want it to end."

"Come. It won't be the last time."

With those words that I read as a promise for more, my body trembles and my balls draw up. "Oh yes. Yes. Fuck."

"That's it," he moans.

Cum shoots from my cock, dripping over my fist and landing on the ground beneath my feet. My body shakes and my breath comes in hard pants.

He pulls out, his cock already softening, and spins me around. His eyes bore into mine as he holds my chin between his thumb and forefinger.

"Thank you, for my gift."

My lips curl up on one end. "Thanks for mine."

It's hours later when we're finally done cleaning up. The body has been removed from the basement, taken deep into the woods behind my house, and dropped into a forgotten and abandoned well.

Both of us have showered, and now we sit on opposite ends of my couch. His phone buzzes in his pocket, so he pulls it out and reads the screen. It's damn near four in the morning. An odd hour for anyone to text.

He sighs and then types out a reply.

"Let me guess," I say. He huffs. "Hey, if you get to be jealous, why can't I?"

"I'm not jealous."

"No? You were fine with that man touching me? What if I told you he sucked my dick? You'd be okay with that?"

He inhales through his nose. "I'd regret not cutting his fucking tongue out, but it's fine."

I snort. "You don't want me with anyone else, do you? You secretly like that I'm so into you."

His brow lifts. "Are you? So into me?" he teases.

"If it's not noticeable by now, I'm not sure what else I'd have to do. Maybe bring good ol' Jason to my basement?"

His eyes narrow. "Jason is in love with some girl. He's not into me."

"Are you into him?"

"No."

"Okay. I guess I believe you."

With a soft exhale, he stands up, rubbing his forehead. "I better get going."

"You don't want to stay? It's late."

He gives me a look, studying my face for several seconds. "No, I'll be fine. I don't do sleepovers."

"You're pretty detached from your emotions, aren't you?" I ask, settling into the couch while I stretch my leg along the cushions.

"Aren't you?"

"I'm not empathetic, but I can form emotional attachments to people."

"Unhealthy attachments."

I smile. "If you say so."

He sighs and heads for the door. "I'll see you around."

"Will you? Or will *I* see *you*?"

His steps come to a stop, but he doesn't turn around, just pauses briefly before walking away.

FIFTEEN

I t's hard liking a psychopath. They're cold and usually don't have the ability to recognize what their actions have done to someone. They don't see the suffering, and if they do, they rarely feel bad about it.

Am I a psychopath? No. Some might say I'm socio-pathic, which is definitely the better of the two if you ask me, but I'm not a fan of labels. I'm just me. Sure, I'm able to take peoples' lives, but it's not like I always wanted to. I had to. If it's you or me, I choose me. In the case of Theo, which was the name of the man Quintin just killed, I *had* to do that.

You see, Quintin wasn't understanding. He thought he wanted me to stay away, but that's not true. He does want me. I had to show him why. He needed this and I provided it. Was it selfish? Sort of, but it was mostly selfless. Which is why it's frustrating that it's been three days and I haven't heard a peep from him.

What else does he want me to do? Do I need to continu-ously present him with gifts? Does he want me to work for his attention and affection? Because I'll fucking do it. While he was brutally fucking my mouth, he said I didn't know what I had done. I assumed he meant I opened a can of worms. That he'd be over every fucking day unable to keep his hands off me. He thanked me, sure. With words. But that's not really enough.

I see him at the coffee shop, chatting with the waitress like they're best friends. I watch him go to the Thai restaurant and gossip with the waitress there. At work, he disappears inside, talks to a girl at the counter, then heads out with a crew. At night, he settles into his house, windows closed, and does something mundane probably. I can imagine him watching *Wheel of Fortune* while eating a sandwich. That's the life he wants? To fit in with society?

On the fourth day since fucking me next to his victim, he emerges from his house, heads to work, and then surprisingly goes to lunch with the woman he works with. He's never done this before. He typically eats alone. Sometimes he doesn't leave the building at all, other times he drives to a fast food place, sits in a lot to eat, then goes back.

He gets in her car, both of them laughing. She drives ten minutes away to a café called Tossed that only offers wraps and salads. Luckily for me, they sit near the window. She reaches out and lays her hand on his, her head thrown back as she cackles. What's so funny? Is *he* funny? I'm sure the version she gets is, but I prefer the version I get. She gets Ezra. I get Quintin.

Ezra stands and walks away. The woman looks down at her phone, glances in the direction Ezra went, smiles, and then her head swivels to look out the window. She's pretty. Not the usual type I go for. For one, she's a brunette, and I've always liked my women blonde. She's young, but not too young. Old enough to not be naive. Maybe close to thirty.

When Ezra returns, he places their food on the table between them. *Such a gentleman.*

Is he dating her? Are they fucking? Maybe just friends? Hard to tell. He hasn't really made a move, but she touches him constantly. I think it may be one-sided here, but I could definitely understand if he wanted to fuck her.

She removes her jacket and her full breasts nearly fall out of her blouse. She looks embarrassed before she buttons the top two that came undone. A calculated move. She wanted him to look at her. To want her.

When they're done eating, they step outside and linger in front of the building. She touches his arm. He smiles. She says something, ducking her head slightly. He reaches out and lifts her chin and replies. She beams.

My bisexuality is raging. He's effortlessly sexy, plus I know what his dick feels like. But she's hot too, and watching them together both fuels my jealousy, but also makes me want to see more. What would he look like fucking her? Would she wrap those pouty lips around his cock and gag on him?

When I snap out of my daydream, I notice she's walking away, popping into a store a couple buildings down. Ezra strolls in the opposite direction, zipping his jacket up. He pulls out a cigarette and lights it, leaning against the stop light at the corner. It's then, when he's alone, that his eyebrows drop, his lips droop in the corners, and he exhales, happy to not be putting on show.

He only gets thirty seconds before a man approaches him from the other side of the street.

Is that Will?

They talk for a good couple of minutes, Ezra's back to me. The other man looks happy. He smiles and laughs, and then pats Ezra on the shoulder. His hand lingers too long.

He walks past Ez, heading in my direction but on the opposite side of the road. I get a good look at him and try to figure out if I've seen him before.

He's attractive if you like pretty boys. Soft skin. Clean cut hair. A tucked in shirt. No thanks.

But then Ezra calls out to him with a *"Hey."* He takes several steps to catch up, and now I can see his face. He's smiling again, but I don't think it's real. I've only ever seen him with a wicked smirk. A snarl. What is Ezra's real smile? Is this man making him smile?

Anger rises in my chest, my heart throwing itself against my ribs with vicious, rapid beats. My skin bristles with red hot rage. I'm so caught up in my own fury, I don't pay attention to their interaction. I begin to focus on him—the object of Ezra's attentiveness.

I wasn't playing around when I told him I couldn't handle him being with another man. A woman? That *might* excite me. If I get to watch. A man? No way in fucking hell. I'm the only man he needs. I'm the only man who can handle him. He can play with a woman. Feel her wet little pussy, squeeze her tits. It's fun. But to think he's manhandling another guy? Stroking his dick and fucking his mouth? I don't fucking think so.

When Mr. Tucked In Shirt leaves. I follow.

EZRA

SIXTEEN

Another Saturday night just means settling in with a book and a strong drink. I don't make plans for weekends. I try to avoid them if I can. So when my phone buzzes with a text just as I take my first sip and crack open said book, I find myself annoyed.

WILL: *Hey! Don't kill me, but do you have plans for tonight? I know you mentioned hating last minute plans, but well, this wasn't planned.*

I SIGH and take a full minute before deciding to respond. She's right. I hate plans in general, but especially last minute plans. It doesn't give me enough time to prepare for whatever I'm about to endure. Before I can reply, another message pops up.

. . .

WILL: *Jason said you have to come out. He said he has to tell you something. He's begging. Lol.*

Will: *You can say no, but we'd like to have you join us. We're at The Hideout.*

I WAIT ANOTHER COUPLE MINUTES, contemplating what I want to do.

ME: *Sure! Sounds like fun. See you later.*

IT WON'T BE FUN, but maybe something will finally happen tonight. I went a long time without having sex, and now that I've just fucked Kaspian last week, I'm already a fiend. It's like the first sip of alcohol after having been sober. Now you want to binge.

It doesn't take me long to get ready. I was already showered, so I only need to put on some different clothes, a spray of cologne, and then I'm out the door.

The time on my dash reads seven past ten and I can't help but wonder what the hell Kaspian is up to. I know it drives him crazy that I don't text him, but I like him crazy, and he likes to work for it. We're both getting what we want, even if he hasn't figured that out yet.

If we fell into traditional dating roles where we text each other every day, hang out all the time and go out for dinner, I'd likely kill him and then myself. I don't want that. He doesn't either. He has the need to obsess and hunt. I keep him guessing and yearning. If I fell to my knees for him so easily, he'd hate it. Kaspian needs me exactly the way I am.

AN HOUR into being at The Hideout and Jason's already told me about how he ran into Samantha and they ended up having lunch together. As friends. But he swears it was a step in the right direction, telling me about his subtle flirting and how she blushed and seemed into it. He plans on anonymously sending her a screenshot of the messages he has between her boyfriend, BJ, and some other girl he's been talking to. I didn't bother to ask how he acquired these messages, because I don't care, but I root for him anyway.

Some guy approaches Willow, obviously into her, but she dismisses him with kindness. Her friend, Cora, is aghast.

"Why didn't you jump on that?" she screeches. "Did you see those cheekbones? The size of his hands? My god."

Willow smiles and shakes her head. "Just keeping my options open." Her eyes fall on me for a few seconds and I get the message loud and clear.

Jason winks at me again, nodding his head as if to give me permission.

Don't get me wrong, Willow's hot, but fucking her would require a lot of control on my end. She seems like the type that wants it slow and soft. Romantic. She's not gonna let me fuck her hard from behind while I yank on her hair. She'd never allow me to come on her face or tits. I like sex rough and dirty, but I suppose I could make it work if I needed to. I haven't felt the inside of a woman in a while.

Problem is...Kaspian. I remember what it was like to be with him, and that's what I crave. He feeds my animalistic nature.

We're not together, though.

Thirty minutes later, Willow decides we should all do body shots. Considering there's only four of us, she's quick to pair us together while Jason and Cora team up.

"Where do you want to lick me?" she whispers in a husky tone, surprising me.

I raise a brow as I take the shot of tequila she hands me. "Where would I get the most flavor?"

She flushes, a slight shiver running down her spine. She clears her throat. "Well, if only we weren't in public, I might be able to show you."

Willow stands before me as I stay seated on the edge of the booth. Jason and Cora have already taken their shots and scurried off to the dance floor, leaving us alone.

"Show me anyway."

She looks nervous, her cheeks turning pink as she looks around. Nobody's paying attention to us. There are quite a few people here, and most of them are drunk at the bar or dancing. It's dark, with only flashes of bright LED lights cutting through the room.

Willow's wearing a casual, long sleeved black dress that stops mid-thigh, and black pantyhose that cover her legs. After another glance around, she slowly lifts the material and rests her hand on her pussy, showing me the black panties under the sheer material.

"Here."

"Hmm."

She lets the material fall back down, and I shift, sitting sideways in the booth as I grab her thigh, bringing her foot to rest beside me.

Her breath catches in her throat as she watches me. My fingers crawl up her leg, finding the crease between her thigh and groin, and then I rip the pantyhose.

Willow gasps as my finger presses against her bare flesh, tearing the hole a little wider. I lean forward and lick her soft skin, making sure to take my time.

"Oh god," she whispers, her hand falling to my head.

I ease back and grab the small dish of salt before I pour it over the spot on her inner thigh. Most of it spills to the floor, but enough clings to my saliva on her skin, and to be honest, I don't give a shit about the salt.

I bring the glass of tequila to my lips and swallow it down before leaning in again and licking the salt from her flesh. When I pull away, she drops her foot and brings the lime to her mouth, placing the wedge between her lips. I stand and bite into it, but don't pull away too quickly.

When I'm done, I toss the rind to the table, and we stay locked in on each other for several seconds.

"Guess it's my turn," she says, her voice airy and soft.

I sit back in the booth, this time moving to the back where it curves. I stretch my arms out along the back, waiting for her to crawl in next to me.

On her knees at my side, her eyes flicker from the hem of my shirt to my neck, deciding what she wants to do. I expect her to do something tame—my wrist, maybe collarbone, but I don't expect for a second for her to lift my shirt. But that's what she does.

I slouch down a little more and she pushes my shirt up to my chest before gazing into my eyes. When I don't object, she leans down and her pink tongue slides out from between her full lips and dances across the bottom of my stomach, right above the waistband of my jeans.

She pinches salt between her fingers and sprinkles it on my skin. After handing me the other wedge, she grabs the shot glass and drinks it down while staring into my eyes. I put the slice of lime in my mouth and watch as her head lowers into my lap, her tongue cleaning up the salt while also dipping lower, beneath the material of my underwear.

I want to put my hand on the back of her head and force her there, make her suck my cock right here and now. She raises her head, eyes full of sinful thoughts as she comes forward to take the wedge. When she sits back, squeezing more of the lime juice into her mouth, my eyes travel over her shoulder.

Across from us, on the other side of the dance floor, Kaspian sits in his own booth, joined by a couple of women, but his eyes are trained on me. The smile starts slowly, his lips taking their time to stretch upwards. He lifts a hand and waves with his fingers.

SEVENTEEN

" I 'm gonna go get some of this salt out of my pantyhose," Willow says with a nervous giggle.

I give her a small grin. "Okay."

My eyes fly back to Kaspian. He just sits there, watching me. I think he'll come over right away, asking about who I'm with, but he doesn't. He just stares.

Jason slides into the booth, sweaty and breathing hard. "Jesus. Cora never wants to stop dancing. I was finally able to pass her off to somebody else."

I pull my gaze from Kaspian. "Oh yeah? I try to avoid the dance floor."

"I don't blame you. Saw a little action going on over here," he says with a grin.

I shake my head. "Don't start."

"I knew something was gonna happen between you two."

"Nothing has."

"Oh please. Does she have to beg you?" My brow arches on its own accord. Jason starts cracking up, leaning over to shove me in the shoulder. "Fucking dog."

"I thought that was you." I look up and find Kaspian next to the table. I see the annoyance burning deep in his eyes.

"Hey," I say, peering up at him. "How long have you been here?"

"A while," he says with a shrug. "An hour maybe." He eyes Jason. "I'm Kas," he says, introducing himself to Jason with an extended fist.

Jason bumps it. "I'm Jason. I think I've seen you around."

"Probably," he answers with a friendly smile. "Small town."

"Tell me about it."

Kaspian sits down next to me, pushing his thigh into mine. "So, what're you two up to tonight? Y'all doing anything after this?"

Jason shakes his head. "Probably not. We got a couple of girls here with us. They'll probably wanna stay."

"I got a couple of girls too," he says, gesturing to his table.

"All to yourself?" Jason asks with wide eyes.

"If I'm lucky," Kas answers, knocking his knee into mine. "Unless you're interested in joining us?"

Jason sputters out a nervous laugh. "Oh. Yeah, I don't know about that."

He's blushing, and of course Kaspian could get him to blush.

"It could be fun. We could swap, unless you're only interested in me." He winks at him, and Jason's ears turn red as he fidgets, running his palms against his jeans.

I squeeze Kaspian's thigh under the table, warning him to cut it out. He drops his hand and pushes mine to his dick. I squeeze, making him squirm.

Jason can hardly get his words out. "I'm not..." He laughs. "I'm not into guys, but thanks. I think." He rubs his hands over his face. "Sorry, I've never been propositioned by a guy before."

Kas turns his head and looks at me, relief in his eyes. "What about you?"

Before I can answer, Willow and Cora show up. Willow looks surprised by the new person at our table, if not slightly annoyed that he's taken her spot next to me. Cora looks delighted by his presence.

"Well, well, well. Who do we have here?" she asks, pushing Willow into the booth so she can sit directly in front of Kaspian.

Kas turns on his charm, smiling and extending his hand to her. "I'm Kas. And who are you two beautiful ladies?"

Cora slips her hand into his. "We're Cora and Willow."

"Willow," Kaspian says slowly, emphasizing *will*. "And Cora," he adds. "Nice to meet you both."

"So, you two are friends?" Willow asks, gesturing between us.

Kaspian looks at me, a smile playing on his lips. "Kinda."

"He fixed my phone recently," I say.

Kas rolls his eyes. "He's using me for my skills." Cora giggles. "We met not that long ago, though. Bonded over the fact that neither of us are from here."

"You might be the only two," Jason says. "Besides the tourists who show up for skiing in the winter, we don't get many transplants."

"Where are you from, Kas?" Willow asks.

"Maine," he answers easily. "I was moving around a while, trying to figure out where I wanted to settle, and then I came across this town."

"And you wanted to stay?" Cora asks with surprise. "That's crazy."

"I never said I was sane," he flirts, winking at her.

She smiles and folds her arms on the table, leaning forward to push her tits up. "Sane is boring."

"That's what I say," Kas says with glee, laughing to sell it as a joke.

Kas focuses his attention on Willow next. "That's a gorgeous necklace," he tells her.

Willow fingers the green pendant hanging from a gold chain. "Thank you."

"Wait, I have to see that ring," he says, reaching for her hand. "It's so unique."

She gives him her hand, her eyes flickering to mine briefly.

"Oh, us and a couple other of our friends went through a DIY jewelry phase. Willow made that ring. We made all sorts of stuff. Rings, earrings, bracelets," Cora rattles off.

He holds her hand delicately as he inspects the jewelry.

"I used gold wire to create the band, and this is a green aventurine gemstone, but I also have them with obsidian and rose quartz." She laughs. "Probably more. You don't want to see my jewelry box."

"Maybe I do," he says softly before easing back.

Willow tucks her hair behind her ear, gaze bouncing between us. He's got her in his grasp already. All he has to do is sink his talons into her.

For the next thirty minutes, Kaspian talks to everyone at the table, answering their questions, making them laugh, and then leaves just to return with a round of shots. He completely forgets about the girls he was with earlier, and they eventually leave.

Cora gets asked to dance by a guy, and shortly after,

Jason decides to leave. The three of us remain at the table, and Kaspian says, "Well, I didn't mean to be the third wheel here."

Willow giggles, her eyes a little glassier thanks to the liquor. "You're not. It's fine."

Kas raises his brows at me. "Well, good. I mean, I always say the more the merrier anyway."

"Me too!" Willow squeals.

"And three is the perfect number," he adds, giving her a pointed look.

She studies me before getting lost in Kaspian's spell again. "I think so too." Her eyes roam my face. "What about you, Ezra?" she asks before sinking her teeth into her bottom lip.

A pregnant pause follows before I say, "I think it's perfect."

Her eyes light up, relieved by my answer. She's been worried this whole time. She likes me, but she's attracted to him too. I'll admit, it's hard to fight the magnetism of his charisma, even if it is fake, so I don't blame her. Afterall, it's why he's so good at what he does. If it wasn't for me, she'd quickly become another victim.

Cora arrives at the table in tears. "Willow, can we go? I want to go home."

"What happened?" she asks, standing up to hold her friend's hands.

"I don't want to talk about it right now. Please, can we go?"

Willow looks back at us, disappointment on her face, but she's a good friend and Cora will come before a possible threesome. "See you guys later."

"Text me and let me know you got home safely," I tell her.

She smiles. "I will."

Kaspian sighs. "So, Will is Willow and Jason's clearly never had a flirtatious encounter with a man."

I shake my head. "I told you."

"You didn't tell me about Willow."

"Maybe I wanted you to stay a little jealous."

His lips twitch. "Why don't you text me?"

"Because I know it drives you crazy, and because I know you'll always come find me."

A growl rumbles in his throat. "You know I love the chase."

EIGHTEEN

"What do you say we head back to Tabu Dreams?" Kas asks.

"The fetish club?" I ask. He nods. "Why?"

"It's not in town," he says slowly, giving me a look that drips with depravity.

"I see." My pulse spikes. "Yeah, why not?"

We leave The Hideout immediately. Kaspian's already dressed in black—a thin sweater clinging to his torso. He probably already planned to go, but I'm in a white and blue color block shirt and a pair of blue jeans, so I have to stop by my house to change first.

Kaspian walks around to the passenger side of my truck, inviting himself to ride with me. I hesitate and stare at him through the window.

He looks amused when he watches me, his lips forming a small grin. "If you think I don't already know where you live, you underestimate me."

I unlock the doors and he slides in, smiling at me.

"I'm not that interesting to watch."

"I disagree, but I'd like to request you leave your blinds open from time to time. Maybe the ones in your bedroom."

I shake my head and start up the truck. It doesn't take too long to get to my house, and when I pull into the driveway, I open the garage and leave the keys in. "I'll be right back."

Kaspian doesn't respond.

After walking through the garage door and into the kitchen, I turn right and travel through the living room before I hit the stairs and make my way to my room. I strip out of my clothes and pull out a pair of black jeans and a T-shirt to match. I top it off with a Pologize business jacket that has a standing collar. It's thin and nice enough to stay comfortable in all night.

After putting on my shoes, I adjust my bracelet and study the jewelry on my dresser. After a few seconds, I decide to put on the necklace with the vial pendant.

I turn off the light at the bottom of the stairs and walk back through my house and enter the garage. Kaspian's not in the passenger seat anymore.

Stalking forward, I look around the area, wondering where the hell he went. Within seconds, I hear the crunch of dead leaves and twigs under approaching footsteps. He appears to the right of the truck, coming from the back area of the house which only leads to a handful of trees.

"What the fuck were you doing?"

"Taking a piss." He looks me up and down. "You look good."

"Let's go," I say, jumping back into the truck.

"You don't take compliments well."

"I could pretend, if that's what you want, but I thought you liked me for who I really am."

"I do."

"Then don't expect me to blush over your words. I can't believe half of them anyway."

He laughs. "I'm at my most honest when I'm with you, and you can one hundred percent believe that I find you attractive."

I ignore him, reversing into the street. It's quiet for a few minutes before he speaks again.

"Do you find me attractive?"

His tone is light and teasing. He's pretending it's just a playful question, but when I glance at him, I can see the eagerness in his eyes. He really wants the answer. He needs it.

"I fucked you, didn't I?"

"Yeah, you did. But I wonder if it was because of the gift I gave you, or because you actually wanted to. Does killing turn you on? The sight of blood? Or is it my face and cock that did it for you?"

"Why does it have to be one or the other?"

He goes quiet, deep in thought. When he speaks again, I don't expect the words. "I take it you're not out."

My eyebrows knit together as my head swivels in his direction. "What the fuck are you talking about?"

"You're bi, aren't you? You fuck both men and women, but nobody here knows that, do they?"

"Nobody knows any of my business."

"So you'll never let anyone see us together."

His voice is changing, taking on that angry, jealous tone. It's how he got when explaining why he had to kill his girlfriend. She didn't appreciate him and everything he did for her. He didn't feel loved and he snapped.

I pull over, parking in the grass on the side of the road. I step out of the truck, making my way to his side. He looks surprised and confused when I rip open his door and yank him from the seat, shoving him against the truck.

With one hand on his chest and my finger in his face, I say, "Do not pull that clingy, obsessive shit with me, you hear me? I am not one of your girlfriends. I'm not a victim of your fucking predatory ways. I'm here with you right now because I want to be, not because you manipulated the situation. I will not bow down to you simply because you want me to."

His eyes are wide as he watches me.

"I will not love you, Kaspian. It's not in me to love anybody. Do not expect it of me." His chin dips the tiniest fraction. "Do you want me to pretend? Do you want me to act the way I do when I let people see what I want them to see? I can smile at you like you're the prettiest thing I've ever seen. If you want a version of me that other people get, I can look you in the eye and tell you you're the best person I've ever met." I bring my forefinger and thumb to his chin, holding it in my grip. "But if you want me—the real me, the one only you and my victims have ever seen, then you'll take me the way I give myself to you, and you won't fucking complain about it."

"Okay," he says in a whisper.

"And I don't give a shit if people know I fuck guys."

I turn to walk away, but he's quick. He grabs my arm and pulls me into him. "What if I said I think I'm already obsessed with you?"

My lips pull up on one end. "I'd say it's not a surprise, but don't expect the same."

KASPIAN

CHAPTER
NINETEEN

I'm here with you because I want to be.

The words play on a loop in my head, making me smile. I have to hide my joy from him, because he'll wonder what the hell I'm so happy about. I heard everything else he said, but I'm listening to this. This is all I want.

He thinks I want him to love me, but I don't. I don't need his love. I need his attention. And he still doesn't realize that he is here because of my manipulation, but he doesn't need to understand. I do.

"What's your plan?" he asks as we approach the bar.

"What do you mean?"

He gives me an annoyed look. "You know why we're here."

"To watch people fuck? To have people watch us fuck? God, I hope it's the last one."

Ezra turns and smiles at the bartender when he takes his drink. "Thank you."

"You new here?" the guy behind the bar asks while he makes my drink.

"Second time," Ezra answers, taking a sip. "Oh, that's good."

The bartender, with his perfectly coiffed hair, grins. "Thank you. I'm so glad you like it."

"Oh, are you?" I ask, staring daggers at him.

His eyes snap to mine, and then Ezra's head turns. He reaches out and clasps his hand around my forearm, his eyes narrowing, giving me a warning.

I cock my head before I slowly turn and face the bartender, giving him a tight, forced smile. "I can't wait to see how mine tastes."

Ezra squeezes me again before releasing his grip. Once I have my drink, I walk away from the bar to find a seat where I can't see the bartender's fucking face. To my dismay, Ezra doesn't immediately follow me. Instead, he stays at the bar, talking to the conventionally attractive man who is *so glad* Ezra likes his fucking drink.

My leg bounces under the table as I watch them. Ezra's eyes meet mine. He stares at me for several seconds before aiming a smile in the bartender's direction, then he gets up and struts over.

"Are you trying to make me kill him?"

He leisurely pulls out the chair to sit in, then takes a long, slow gulp of his drink before setting it down on the table.

"Why do you feel threatened?"

"Why do you try to provoke me?"

His lips stretch across his face slightly. "Maybe I want to see you at your worst."

A thrill of excitement runs through me. I lean forward. "Oh yeah? So when you talk to other guys in front of me, like that fucking dickhead," I say, gesturing toward the bar, "and like the guy on the street the other day, you do it because you're thinking about me?"

Some sort of amusement flashes across his face before he asks, "What guy on the street?"

I bite my lip, but it's too late. I've given myself away.

"Kaspian." I remain quiet and he chuckles. "I saw you. I knew you were watching me."

"So, you *were* thinking about me?"

"Hard not to when you follow me from work to a restaurant."

"And you wanted to see what I'd do if I saw you talking to that stuffy fucking clown?"

"I hate that guy. We're not even friends. He's a client who's never satisfied and complains a lot."

"What were you hoping I'd do?" I ask, getting closer to him, my voice dropping.

"I wondered if it would draw you out."

"I followed him," I state. "Once he walked away from you."

Ezra folds his arms on the table. "And what did you do?"

"Not my worst, unfortunately. I followed him to a boutique where he met up with his wife and kids. Figured there was nothing to worry about there."

"Hmm." He takes a sip of his drink and lets his eyes bounce around the room. "So, did you have a plan?"

"Not particularly."

"I like to have plans."

"So, plan."

"I'll work on it. In the meantime, let's look around."

We end up finishing our drinks in the bar area before we make our way to the section with the rooms. In the hallway, we get propositioned by an older couple, but politely decline. In one of the group rooms, we watch as a party of four have a good time together. In another room, there's three people going at it on a couch. After some eavesdropping, we determine two of them are married, and the other guy is the one they invited in. However, it's him who has sex with the woman, while the husband watches.

"You think you could do that?" I ask, leaning into Ezra's side.

"Watch you fuck somebody or fuck somebody in front of you?"

"Watch me with someone else."

He's quiet for a while, digesting the question. "Not sure," he answers.

Not the right answer. He should be livid to watch me be with someone else. Why would he let me fuck around with someone? Wouldn't he be jealous? Angry?

Sure, I could *potentially* watch him with a woman, but that's different. That's my kink, and I know he wouldn't like it more than he likes being with me. But he'd let me go off with someone? I don't think so. He's just like me, but he won't admit it. I keep having to teach him lessons.

When my opportunity comes, I take it, and it comes in the form of a tall, muscled man with dark hair and bronze skin. He's similar to Ezra in those ways, but he lacks Ezra's fierceness.

"Hey guys," the man says with a friendly smile. "I'm Diego. You two having fun tonight?"

"Hi Diego. I'm Kaspian. This is Ezra."

Diego nods at Ezra, who barely reciprocates the gesture, before sliding his eyes to me. Hey, if he can flirt with bartenders, I can do this.

"Are you two together?" Diego asks.

I look over at Ezra. He's relaxed on the couch, his arm slung over the back, dark intense eyes on me.

"We're not in love or anything," I say with a laugh, glancing back at Ezra with a wink. "We don't have a label," I tell Diego. "What about you? Here with anyone?"

"Nope," he says with a grin.

"Interesting," I reply, giving him a quick once over, making sure my eyes linger on his biceps and lips.

Diego's eyes flicker to Ezra, but his icy gaze is off-putting. Diego doesn't attempt to flirt with him, instead focusing on me.

After several minutes of talking, some laughing, and plenty of flirtatious touching on my part, Diego clears his throat, aware that Ezra is watching us.

"So, can I assume you're available tonight? Do you want to go to a private room or stay here?" His eyes move to the couch and back.

I look at Ezra, who's barely stirred since Diego arrived, and say, "We were actually just talking about some voyeuristic, cuckolding type stuff."

Diego perks up. "Oh yeah? Cuckolding's quite popular."

I nod. "Yeah, definitely. I think it would be fun." I face Ezra. "What do you think?"

After a few seconds, the corners of his lips lift slightly, something dangerous flashing in his eyes. "Yes. It would be fun."

My surprise at his answer shows on my face when my eyebrows drop and my smile fades, but that's okay. We just have to push this along a little further.

"Let me go use the restroom, and then I'll meet you guys in a private room," Ezra says.

I study him, confused by his reaction. "I'm not sure which room is available."

140

Ezra smiles in a way that forces goosebumps to spread across my skin. "I'll find you."

Diego places his hand on my back and escorts me through the doorway. Lots of rooms are taken, but we eventually find a free one in another hall.

"Drink?" he asks me.

"No alcohol allowed back here."

He pulls a flask from an inner pocket in his jacket. "BYOB."

I laugh. "No, I'm okay."

He removes his jacket and tosses it on a chair before stepping out of his shoes. "Your boyfriend seems a little hostile."

I lay across the bed and lock my hands under my head. "Not my boyfriend."

Diego removes his pants, showing off his impressive size in a small, tight pair of briefs. "Well, your *friend* seems hostile. You sure he'll be okay with this?"

I smirk at him. "If he's not, he'll let us know."

My eyes keep dancing to the door, waiting for Ezra to find us. Diego starts removing my shoes, and then unbuttons and unzips my jeans, pulling them down my legs.

A figure appears in the doorway. Ezra. He pauses for only a second before stepping inside and closing the door. The sound of a chair dragging closer to the bed fills the room before he sits down.

"You sure you're okay with this, man?" Diego asks, already straddling my legs.

Ezra's eyes move from mine to Diego's. "Oh, please." He gestures at me with his hand like I'm a bowl of chips and he's offering one to a guest. "Go ahead." His head swivels back in my direction and I search his eyes for some sort of emotion, but there is none.

141

I remove my sweater, leaving only a T-shirt and underwear on my body, and Diego lies over me, grinding his cock against mine as he brushes his whiskered face across my neck. I plant my feet on the bed, bending my knees and allowing him to settle between them. My hands dance across the muscles in his back, and his fingers thread themselves in my hair.

He kisses my neck, his tongue licking a path across my collarbone as he travels to the other side. I turn my head and find Ezra stoically watching us. He doesn't look turned on or angry. He's watching this happen like he's watching golf on TV.

After the last time we were here and he all but kicked out the guy I was with then, I thought for sure he'd have a stronger reaction now. Maybe he really was only mad because I left him without saying where I was going and not because of what I was doing.

Diego touches, kisses, and licks my body. His erection is hard against my skin as he works to get me in the mood, but I'm too focused on why Ezra doesn't care to even think about getting off. When I find Ez again, he's leaning his head on his hand, his thumb and middle finger cradling his chin while his forefinger stretches across his cheek. He looks deep in thought, but when his eyes finally lock onto mine, he gives me a slight grin.

What the fuck? This is not how I thought this would go.

Diego strips out of his underwear, his cock pointing right at me as he moves to remove my boxers. Ezra's watching my face, a slight lift of his eyebrow as if he's waiting to see what I'll do. I sit up and remove my shirt before lying back down.

Diego gets between my legs, skin to skin, and then his eyes fall to the wound on my chest. It's healing, but it isn't the prettiest thing to look at. It's red and scabbing over.

"What happened?" he asks, fingers reaching for it.

"Just an accident." My eyes cut to Ezra. His jaw ticks.

Diego softly touches the flesh around the wound. "Looks painful." I find Ezra again. He shifts in his seat.

"I'm a big boy. I'll be fine."

He smiles and then leans down, pressing a gentle kiss to the cut. "I'll take care of you."

Ezra is on his feet and Diego presses his lips to the area again, unaware of the movement. He peppers kisses down my torso, heading for my cock.

I watch Ezra as his nostrils flare with angry breaths. *There he is.*

His eyes are menacing and his jaw is tight. "Get rid of him," he mouths silently, and I think of ignoring his demand, just so I can keep seeing this side of him. My brief hesitation sends more fury into his eyes.

"Um," I say, putting my hands on his shoulders. "I might need a minute. Sorry."

Ezra steps back and puts a hand on the back of the chair.

"Oh," Diego says. "Yeah, sure. You okay?"

"I guess I thought I was braver than I am." I give him a coy smile. "Can we have the room for a minute?"

He looks at Ezra who's trying to remove some of the anger of his expression.

"Sure."

He quickly dresses and leaves, possibly embarrassed and annoyed.

Ezra seethes in a way that's quiet and frightening. It's boiling under the surface, but he's not exploding. He's not yelling or acting out.

"Ezra," I start.

He holds up his hand, cutting me off. He walks away, removing his jacket and taking deep, controlled breaths before he opens the door.

Wait, what?

I quickly start pulling on my boxers, but it's not long before he's back, this time followed by another person.

A small twink that's probably just legal enough to be here trails him like a puppy wearing skintight black pants and a black mesh top. He looks like he's never had facial hair in his life, and his lips are pink and glisten from here. His dirty blond hair falls over his brows and I want to rip every strand from his head. One by one.

"We're trying this cuckolding thing," Ezra says with a look in my direction followed by a wink.

"Ezra." My voice is low, his name drawn out in a slow warning.

"How about you get on your knees?" he tells the guy, undoing his pants.

"Yes, sir," the man teases, giddy with excitement. "I'm all about this. I bet I could suck your dick better than he can."

Ezra grins. "Maybe you can."

I'm kneeling in the middle of the mattress, watching as this unfolds. There's no fucking way this is happening. My brain struggles to deal with what I'm seeing. It unfolds in steps.

Ezra's pants are around his ankles. The twink's hands are on his thighs. Ezra reaches into his boxer-briefs and touches himself.

The man on his knees bites his lip, ready and excited. "Let me see that big dick. I want it in my mouth." He looks at me, green eyes bursting with superiority. "You might lose your man after tonight."

I scramble out of the bed and get to my feet.

Reaching up, he tugs Ezra's underwear down, freeing his cock. He licks his lips and lets out a moan. "He probably doesn't know how to handle this. Don't worry, I'll show him."

His fingers wrap around Ezra's shaft.

"Yeah, he does need to be taught a lesson."

Like he's in a fucking porno and putting on a show, he sticks out his strangely long tongue, ready to slap Ezra's cock on it.

I rush forward. They're not far away, and I get there before he can touch his slimy tongue to Ezra's dick. My fingers seize the muscled organ, squeezing and yanking on it with the idea of ripping it from his fucking filthy mouth.

He looks up at me with wide eyes, grunting and trying to pull away from me, but he only hurts himself during the struggle.

When I clasp my other hand around his throat, I let go of his tongue and pull him up to his feet. "No, I'm going to show you that you don't touch what's mine."

I walk him backward until he slams into the wall, and then I reach for the glass bowl filled with condoms on the table next to us and pick it up and shatter it. Glass shards fly everywhere, and I pick up the largest one and hold it to his lips.

"No, please. Oh god," he cries, tears springing from his eyes.

"Let me see that tongue again, pretty boy."

He pins his lips together, turning his head to the side as tears stream down his face. I force the glass between his lips and then I feel Ezra's presence behind me.

His chest touches my back and his mouth stops near my ear. "You can't do this here."

"I will fucking kill him."

"Not here," he says, coming in close and rubbing his nose down the side of my neck. "You're too impulsive."

My chest heaves. "He was going to put your dick in his mouth. He was talking shit."

He inhales deeply, his hands coming to rest on my hips. "Don't start a game you can't see through to the end, Kaspian." His lips touch my ear and he whispers, "I will always win."

A shiver runs down my spine, and the guy in front of us wiggles, trying to get away from my grip. Ezra steps away and returns with the flask Diego must've forgotten in his haste to leave. I watch as he twists a small metal cap off the pendant of his necklace and pours the liquid from the vial into the flask.

He comes around and stops in front of the man, reaching out to gently guide my hand away from his face.

When he no longer has a piece of glass pressed against his lips, he opens his mouth to scream. Ezra shoves the flask between his teeth and effortlessly yanks him down with his other hand, cradling him as he gets him to the floor.

The man coughs and sputters, choking on the liquor. Ezra pulls the flask away momentarily, holding his hand over the man's mouth until he swallows. He does it one more time, pouring the remaining liquid down his throat.

Ezra straddles him, hand clamped over his lips so he can't make any noise.

"What did you give him?"

"GHB."

After about ten minutes, the man's movements slow. He

doesn't try to buck Ezra off of him, and his eyes begin to droop.

Ezra stands up. "We gotta go. They'll just think he got wasted."

"No. We can't leave him here. He could still tell people what happened."

I watch as he rolls over, trying to push himself up, making noises.

"He's had a lot to drink, plus with what I just gave him, he's not going to be capable of making much sense soon. Plus, I never said we were leaving him."

We stare at each other for a few seconds before my lips form a wicked grin. Ezra returns it and makes my heart flutter.

EZRA

TWENTY

After Kaspian gets dressed, we clean up the mess from the shattered bowl, putting the glass in the trash and the condoms in a drawer. Working together, we get the blond guy up on his feet. The drug mixed with alcohol can have serious effects, and it doesn't take long to kick in. Right now, he's drowsy and confused, so we can get away with saying he just had too much to drink. Soon, he could start vomiting or pass out.

Like two good friends, we have his arms around our shoulders as we get him out of the room and into the darkened corridor. Luckily, there aren't many people lingering in the hall. It's not like these rooms are for voyeurs.

"Is there a back exit?" I ask Kaspian.

"Yeah, but you're not supposed to use it. It'll trigger an alarm. We can go out the front. It'll be fine."

The man mumbles a few things as we pass people, but he can hardly form the words correctly or speak coherently. They'll never know he's begging for help. He doesn't have it in him to even look frightened.

"What's going on?" a voice asks as we hit the front door.

"Master Blake," Kaspian says, angling his head over his shoulder.

The man is in black leather pants and a tight black shirt that's sheer down the middle. He looks angry, his pale face set in a scowl as he assesses the situation.

"What's happening here?" he asks again, getting a look at the blond.

"Stupid idiot had drugs on him," Kaspian says. "I walked in on him popping a few pills and downing it with his own liquor."

"Fuck!" the man curses.

"Don't worry," Kaspian says. "We're getting him out of here so it won't fall on you or the club."

"Nick. Is he new?" Master Blake asks, pointing to the bald guard at the door.

Nick pulls out his iPad and does some clicking and scrolling. "Second time here, sir."

"Get rid of everything we have on him. He was never a member and never will be." He turns his gaze back on us. "Thank you, Kaspian."

"Of course," Kas replies with a grin. "We should go soon, though."

The blond's head bobs, dropping low as his chin hits his chest.

"Yeah. Go."

"That was helpful," I say as we get the blond into the truck.

"Yeah. He won't want any backlash or investigations. Nobody will know he was ever there."

"Good thing you have such a good relationship with *Master Blake*."

Kaspian grins at me from the passenger side of my truck as he holds the man up. "I love when you get jealous."

"I'm not jealous. To be jealous would be to have some sort of insecurity or fear. What I feel is something else."

I get in and start up the truck.

Kaspian chuckles. "Okay."

"Where are we going?" I ask, wanting to get off the subject.

"I'll direct you."

WE'RE SURROUNDED BY TREES, miles and miles away from any road. Kaspian said he's been here before, and I don't have to ask why, because I can assume it was for the same reason we're here now. I didn't know this when I chose Vermont to move to, but the land is seventy-six percent forested, giving us plenty of places that most people will never venture to.

Kaspian has the man laid out on the ground and is straddling his chest, making sure he's conscious enough to know what's about to happen.

Watching him is thrilling, but I quickly realize to see him in his true form is to watch him at his most impulsive. He would've cut that man's tongue from his mouth in the room, but I know to be smart. We can't have a crime scene. We can't have blood and screams of terror in such a public place.

I rest my back against the wide trunk of a tree and observe the way he works. He's still angry, but not as angry as he was in the moment, and I vow to make sure he's capable of freeing himself fully next time.

Particularly upset with the man's tongue, he uses my small blade to slice it down the middle. His eyes take on a villainous gleam as the blood pours out and the man writhes beneath him, groaning and screaming.

Kaspian presses his hand to his nose and mouth, and since we don't have to worry about anyone hearing us out here, I know it's not to keep him quiet. He's going to suffocate him with his own blood.

When the man's body goes still and the noises stop, Kaspian removes his hand and stares down at his newest victim. His shoulders rise and fall with deep breaths before he stands up. He still has that look in his eyes. It's one I've never seen before. He's not the carefully constructed Kaspian. He's authentically himself—an impulsive, twisted, obsessive sociopath.

Seeing him like this brings me a sense of joy I've never felt. Like I've found something I've been missing. Not that I think he's my soulmate; I don't believe in that shit. But just knowing he exists and having the luxury of watching him like this makes me feel...relief.

He stalks toward me, hunger in his eyes and blood on his hands. I remain relaxed against the tree and grin at him when he stops in front of me, his body pressing against mine.

"Look what you made me do."

I smirk. "I made you do that? Or did your little game with Diego start this?"

He runs his finger over my cheek. "You didn't seem bothered by what was going on between us until he started touching the place you cut me."

"I was planning."

"Hmm. So, you *don't* want to see me with anyone else?"

"You can do what you want, but you can't be mad about any reaction I may have."

His satisfied smile is back, and then he moves closer, leaning his forehead against mine. "I didn't like seeing him on his knees in front of you. I wanted to tear out his tongue and sling it at the wall."

I hold his face in my hands and pull him away to look in his eyes. "I know."

"Tonight was supposed to be for you."

"I'm not completely disappointed," I say with a crooked smile.

"Completely?"

I drag my teeth across my bottom lip. "I need you to take care of something else," I say, grabbing one of his hands and placing it on my cock.

"Someone's excited," he teases, stroking me through my pants.

"You excite me."

His eyes light up, his face transforming with his glee. He's easy to please while also being quick to anger.

"I want to taste your excitement," he says, lowering himself to his knees, unbothered by the cold and rough ground.

Kaspian shoves my clothing to my ankles and grabs my cock, wrapping his lips around my crown before taking me to the back of his throat, gagging. With skilled actions, he strokes and sucks me off, moaning around my length while also playing with my balls.

After a while, he eases back, my cock falling from his mouth. He then takes me in his hand and strokes while his tongue licks and sucks on my sac. I close my eyes and enjoy the pleasure of his mouth, and then the tip of his tongue reaches further under my balls, dancing across my taint.

"Shit," I curse, reaching for his head.

I drag the back of my shoe against the trunk of the tree, kicking it off and removing one of my legs from the confines of my pants. I shove his face deeper between my legs, allowing him to run his tongue around my hole.

He moans, grabbing my thigh and lifting it up higher so he can properly devour me. I take over stroking my cock as the tip of his tongue dips into my ass.

"Fuck," I grunt.

"Mm," he murmurs, fingertips digging into my skin.

My fist moves up and down my shaft with vigor, and as soon as I feel the orgasm building, I thread my fingers through his hair and yank his head away.

He stares up at me, his mouth open, saliva glistening across his lips and chin, and specks of blood splattered on his face like freckles. "Fucking beautiful," I say with a groan before stepping forward, "Show me your tongue."

He listens, flattening it while also having the sides fold up slightly. I release my load into his waiting mouth, the white cum pooling together in the center, while some slides deeper into his mouth or drips down his chin.

"Fuck yeah," I say, my tone husky.

I take my cock and shove it back in his mouth, sliding it across the cum and pushing it to the back of his throat.

He swallows and moves his mouth up and down my shaft a few more times, making sure he gets every last drop.

"So fucking good," he says, wiping his mouth as he stares up at me.

"I was gonna say the same thing. Now come here."

He stands up and waits to hear what I say next. I undo his pants and shove them, along with his boxers, down to his mid-thigh. His dick is already mostly hard and I wrap my fingers around his shaft, eliciting a gasp and moan from him.

"Do you want to come?"

He nods. "Oh yeah."

I stroke him slowly, teasing his head with my fingertips. "Do you think you deserve to come?"

He groans low in this throat. "Yes."

"Even after you got naked with Diego?" My hand halts its movement, but my fingers stay wrapped around him.

Kaspian whimpers. "I did it for you."

"You did it for yourself."

He shakes his head, eyes closed, hips rocking as he fucks my fist. "No."

"You wanted me to watch him fuck you?"

"No. I wanted you to stop him."

"Did you want his cock?" I ask, gripping his dick tighter.

"No, I didn't."

"Whose dick did you want?"

"Yours. Fuck, Ezra," he moans.

"Mm. When we're alone, call me Quintin. That's who I am with you."

"Ah fuck."

I push him back and spit on his cock, returning to my movements. I put my other hand around his throat, squeezing slightly as I jerk him.

He rests his forearm on the trunk behind me, his temple pressed against my forehead. He drags his cheek against mine and then his lips are on my neck, planting soft kisses.

"You don't know how much you turn me on. Fuck. Having your hands on me...Jesus, Quintin. It's all I want."

"You don't want my cock, Kaspian? Just my hands?"

"Your cock is fucking spectacular." He moans, his hand gripping my waist. "I want you anyway I can get you. I want everything."

"I know you do. You're so fucking greedy. So needy for me, aren't you?"

"Yes!" he cries out, thrusting his hips.

156

"What about my mouth, Kaspian?" I ask in a whisper, letting my lips brush against the shell of his ear. "Do you want to fuck my mouth?"

"Oh shit. I want it so bad," he mutters, back bowing as he sinks his teeth into a chunk of flesh in my neck.

I let out a hiss. "Fuck!"

"I want it. I want it. I want it," he chants. "Ah. Oh god. Quintin."

"Make a mess. Let me feel that hot cum on my hand."

He cries out, body shaking as his sweat-slicked forehead rests against mine. Warmth spills over my fist and hits my thigh.

"Oh my god," he says with a shaky breath.

His hand comes up and rests on the side of my face, and then he opens his eyes and steps back. "Well, I think we're starting to develop a habit."

"What do you mean?"

"We kill and then we come."

I snort, shaking my head.

We start to pull our clothes on and I wipe my hand and thigh with one of my socks before I put my foot back in my shoe and tuck the sock in my pocket.

"Is that the only time we'll fuck or jack each other off?" he asks.

I lift my head and look at him. "No. Murdering someone doesn't get me off. Not like you think."

His brow arches like he doesn't believe me. "Hmm."

"You think that's why I fucked you before? Because killing that guy got me turned on? Or seeing his dead body?" I ask, gesturing to the corpse twenty feet away.

He cocks his head. "So what is it?"

I shake my head and stare up into the sky, shoving my hands in my jacket pockets. When I lower my chin, I stare into his eyes. I suppose he's partially right. "Even if the blood and violence is excitable to me, you could show up to my house on a random Tuesday and I'd still fuck you."

He bites down on his lip before giving me a wide grin. "I see."

"We have some work to do," I say, walking toward my truck. "Luckily, I have some landscaping tools."

"Okay, cool."

I remove two shovels and hand him the garden spade. "Does killing someone turn you on?" I ask as we walk back toward the body.

Kaspian looks at me with a bewildered expression. "No. I'm not some sort of sicko."

We both start laughing.

TWENTY-ONE

Holding me to my word, Kaspian shows up at my house on Tuesday, and I bend him over my couch and fuck him until he comes on my floor. Luckily, it's hardwood.

Wednesday and Thursday go by without any communication, but our pseudo-relationship doesn't require us to be in constant contact.

When Friday rolls around, Willow asks me to go to lunch with her again. I agree because the whole week has been a little awkward. More on her part than mine. I'm assuming she's embarrassed by our conversation at the club with Kaspian, or possibly about the body shots we did off each other.

We go back to the same place—Tossed. She orders a grilled chicken salad and I get a southwestern chicken wrap. As soon as I take my first bite, she puts her fork down.

"Okay, so let's address the elephant."

I use a napkin to wipe the corner of my mouth, but since my mouth is full, I don't speak. I raise my eyebrows at her and nod, gesturing for her to go ahead.

"Last weekend." I nod again, still chewing. "How close are you and Kaspian?"

The question catches me off guard, but I hold up a finger and finish swallowing my food before I answer.

"We're friends, I suppose. We don't talk every day, but we hang out occasionally."

I don't know why I didn't tell her that we also hookup, and if Kas was here to notice that omission, he'd probably lose his shit.

She nods, chewing on her bottom lip nervously. "Was that conversation weird for you?"

"What conversation?"

She buries her face in her hands. "Please don't make me repeat it."

I chuckle. "I'm going to guess *the more the merrier*."

"Yes," she mumbles into her hands.

I reach out and pull one of her hands down. "Look at me."

She hesitantly looks up, cheeks inflamed. "Sorry."

"Don't be. It's fine."

"Do you look at me weird now?"

"Of course not."

"I didn't want to put you in an awkward place with your friend, and honestly, I was just all over the place. Stupid alcohol. I suppose you can guess that I'm kinda into you."

I grin. "Maybe."

"But you seem sort of into me too."

"Maybe," I say with a wink, giving her the reaction she wants.

She rolls her eyes, a smile playing on her lips. "But..." I'm left hanging as she brings her thumb to her mouth, biting at her nail. "Well, Kaspian..."

I lift my chin and watch her sort through the words in her head until she figures out how to arrange them into her next sentence.

I think she'll bring up the idea of a threesome. She'll ask if I'd be okay with that. She'll wonder if it'll affect our friendship or working relationship. She won't want things to be weird between us, but she wants to do it anyway.

I'm not beyond thinking that people can't have sex without forming attachments. Maybe it's me because I've never really been able to form healthy attachments. The sex I've had in my life is purely carnal. It's a need to be fulfilled. I don't have the need to be loved.

However, Kaspian's the first person I've felt a sense of possession over.

"I ran into him the other day."

My brows lift. "You did?"

She nods. "Yeah. We talked for a little while."

It's my turn to nod. "That's nice."

"Yeah." She plays with the straw in her water. "He asked me out."

My shock is hard to conceal. My head tilts, eyes widen, and my brows reach for my hairline. "Oh really?"

"I said yes."

She watches me carefully, looking for any signs that scream I'm not happy about it.

"Oh okay. Where are you going?"

"Um. I'm not sure yet. He didn't tell me. He's going to call me and let me know."

"I see."

"But, yeah, I just wanted to let you know." She pauses. "I already know you pretty well." *Not really.* "And I like you. But I don't know him."

"Okay?" It's a question because I don't know where she's going with this.

"I'm still very much a believer in *the more the merrier*," she says, giving me a look. "But now that I'm sober, I think it's better that I at least know him a little more before even doing that."

I give her a small smile. "I see. I get it."

"Okay," she says with an exhale. "I feel better."

"Good."

"Let's eat."

THE REST OF THE AFTERNOON, my mind is spinning with theories and churning with questions. She said she ran into him, but if I know anything, I know that was probably calculated on his part. He's a stalker. He knows where to find people if he wants to. I know that's how he ended up at the club that night in the first place.

He asked her out, not the other way around. Why would he do that? If Willow is just wanting to get to know him on a date before jumping into a threesome she's clearly assumed will happen, then what is the reasoning behind him asking her out? It's not like I'm aware of anyone else he may be dating or fucking, but to be honest, I've assumed it was just me. My only issue is I know about his tendency to get fixated on women, and Willow is too close to me to become a victim. I can't have people questioning me about my relationship with her. We work together and we've been seen out together multiple times. I don't want to be looked into too deeply, and that's the only reason he can't choose her as his prey.

My first instinct is to confront him and simply ask, but I

keep myself from being hasty. I'll find out on my own, which is how I end up outside a small shop on Saturday evening. Willow texted me excitedly about where their date would be. Apparently he's taking her to a sip and paint class.

I was hoping it would be easier to spy and eavesdrop, but unfortunately, the shop they're holding this class in isn't very big, and you have to reserve a spot, so I won't be able to get in anyway.

Instead, I hang out across the street under a small over-hang that covers the recessed door of a women's boutique. It only doesn't look too strange because the rain is pouring down and everybody is seeking cover hoping it'll slow down. I have an umbrella to both protect myself from the rain, and to keep my face from being seen.

I watch as Kaspian parallel parks half a block away. He goes around to her side with an umbrella and opens the door, attempting to shield her from the rain. They laugh as they jog down the street, holding on to each other as the wind whips the rain into their faces. It's a scene out of a fucking romcom.

Willow walks through the door while Kaspian closes the umbrella, but he follows her inside shortly after. I can only see them through two rectangular window cutouts in the door. They're laughing while Kaspian shakes water from his hair. They're only there for a minute, just long enough for Willow to remove her coat and put her hair into a ponytail, then they walk away and head to the class that I don't have access to.

I know this particular class is three hours long, so it gives me time to visit Kaspian's house before I need to be back to see where they go next.

IT'S NOT hard to get into his house. Removing a screen is nothing, and his window was unlocked. Inside, I look everywhere I can to find any bit of information about Kaspian. My main reason for wanting to get to know him was because I wanted to know why he is the way he is. He told me about previous girlfriends and what made him snap, but something has to happen to you to get you to that point, right? Sociopaths—and I truly believe he is one—are typically created with some sort of trauma in their childhood.

While I suppose it doesn't matter why, I'm still curious as to how we ended up the way we are, and now I'm probably interested in him in more ways than one.

My personal experience is different. My mom and dad were decent people. They owned a couple of local mom and pop grocery stores, so we had a good amount of money. We lived in a nice neighborhood surrounded by kind neighbors. I had nearly everything I wanted. I was an only child, so it could get boring, but I couldn't complain too much.

We always had food to eat, even if it wasn't together. Mom and Dad worked late sometimes, and I'd be with a babysitter until they thought I was old enough to be left alone, which was probably around eleven. But I always felt a little sad, even if there wasn't anything to be sad about. Eventually, that sadness turned into anger and frustration. I acted out, but my parents didn't really do much. They chalked it up to being a preteen boy who was likely starting puberty.

Later, I'd overhear whispered conversations about me. They were concerned when I beat up a boy in the neighborhood. However, I lied and said he started it and I was defending myself. They could understand self-defense, but the boy was hurt pretty badly. Truth is, he didn't do anything but look at me weird and whisper something to his friend. I snapped, and you know what? Afterward, I felt better. Less sad.

My parents brought up my dad's brother—an uncle I wasn't aware I had. Apparently he had what they called, "mental issues." So they started to wonder if I was like him. Dad seemed concerned about this, so one day I brought up his brother to see what he had to say about him. He looked shocked that I knew about this brother. He questioned how I found out and then got onto me about eavesdropping. He ended the conversation by saying he was dead and not to ask about him again.

When I got into a couple fights at school, they didn't know how to punish me. They said I couldn't go out and play, but that was fine. I hated those kids. They told me no dessert, so I only ate it when they were at work. They told me no TV, but I had books, so I didn't care.

One night, when I was older, maybe about sixteen, I heard my mom tell my dad that she was afraid of me. Afraid of how I looked at her. Thrown off by my lack of emotion. She didn't understand why I didn't cry when her father died. Something about that, about her fear, was thrilling. Powerful.

Eventually, I could see the concern in my dad's eyes. He watched me carefully, even when I was only sitting in a chair and reading. It was like he was always bracing himself for an explosion. I later realized that silence was far scarier than shouting. To see someone boiling with rage but composing themselves and not acting out...it's terrifying; you can only assume they're plotting their revenge. I couldn't hide my anger completely. You saw it in my eyes or the clenching of my fists, but when you don't act the way they expect you to, it throws them off.

Dad tried tough love for a while, thinking raising his voice at me would get me to snap out of it. He wanted me to stop getting in fights and getting suspended from school. He didn't want me out past dark because he didn't trust what I was doing.

When I turned eighteen, I left home and went to college about two hours away. I hated it. I hated the people. Everyone thought they were smarter than everyone else. I hated the athletes who thought they could do what they wanted simply because they were on a team. I hated the girls who flirted with me to get me to help them with their work. I hated the teachers and their uppity attitudes. My rage was growing.

I nearly killed a guy in a bathroom because he asked why I was such a loner. I had to restrain myself, but not until after I punched him in the face. I was two seconds from slamming his head into the sink when someone else walked in.

After that, I overheard some people talking about how weird it was that I was always alone and quiet. Rumors grew from the bathroom incident and turned into something crazier than it was. I knew then I had to be better at fitting in, even if I had to fake it.

By the time I went home for the summer, I was at my breaking point. Then I heard my parents talking about me again. Which was upsetting because I was fine. At least that's what I'd have them believe. I smiled at them and hugged them. I expressed myself more than I ever did when I lived with them, but it turns out they thought *that* was weird. They didn't appreciate my effort and instead believed it to be more alarming. Mom would hardly hug me. Dad avoided me. We didn't eat together; they always had somewhere to be.

I planned and plotted, and that's how I ended up at a girl's house the evening I decided they couldn't live anymore. We went to a party, to be seen. We ate at a diner with a ton of people around. Again, to be seen. I went to her apartment where she lived with a roommate, and the three of us drank some more. Lanie was already three sheets to the wind by the time we went to her bedroom. She hit the bed and was snoring in less than five minutes.

I snuck out the window and walked about three miles; I didn't want my car to be seen and I couldn't ask anybody for a ride. There weren't any guns in the house, probably because they didn't want me to ever get my hands on one, but the kitchen was full of knives.

Dad went first. It was easier than I thought. They both slept like the dead, and Dad barely made a noise when the knife slipped between his ribs. A gasp preceded a groan, and then my hand was over his nose and mouth as he squirmed. Mom woke up and started screaming, so I had to move fast. She didn't run out of the room right away. She was too shocked at the scene playing out in front of her. When she finally got up to flee, I reached over and grabbed her arm and flung her back to the bed. Dad wasn't capable of helping her by that point, and she went the same way as him.

Afterward, I set the scene to make it look like someone broke in. I changed into some new clothes and got rid of my ruined ones on my walk back to Lanie's. They were torn to shreds, drenched in bleach, and thrown in a bag with rocks and dropped into a lake when I crossed the bridge.

I climbed back into bed with Lanie, slept for a few

hours, woke up and took a shower and went back home to find my parents. Of course, I ran to them and touched them, hoping they'd be alive and that's why there was blood on me. I sobbed and expressed confusion and anger. I did everything you're supposed to do.

But I didn't kill them because they traumatized me. I just did it. And that's when I started looking into psychopathy and personality disorders. It's genetics usually. Nothing I could do about it. They didn't get me any help, so who's really to blame?

Kaspian, however, he's different. He's the other side of my coin. Similar, but not quite. After searching through every drawer, cabinet, and cliché hiding place there is, I finally find something. A small locked box hidden in plain sight. I almost didn't even notice it.

On his dresser is a lamp, some cologne bottles, a half empty water bottle, jewelry, a folded shirt, a bowl with random receipts and cards, and a box. It looks like it could be used to hold jewelry.

I find a safety pin amongst the clutter, but it doesn't work to open the lock. I eventually find something in his kitchen to get it open. When I look inside, there are several old photos, some folded papers, and a mini notebook. There's one photo that nearly rips the air from my lungs.

What. The. Fuck.

TWENTY-TWO

I knew not to trust him. I know how people like us survive on lies. It's our life's blood. I'm also aware that he's pretty smart, but I didn't see this coming. I didn't expect this twist.

I had planned on going back to the sip and paint class to see where they went afterward. I had even thought about staying in his house to confront him when he got home, but I wasn't altogether sure that Willow wouldn't be with him. But mostly, I'm aware that being near him right now isn't safe for either of us. I'm too surprised. Angry. Confused. I need time to think and plan.

He texted me Sunday and I ignored it. That won't be too surprising to him, but he'll only put up with it for so long before he shows up.

On Monday, I stop at the front desk and talk with Willow for a few minutes.

"And of course it was raining, so my hair got all frizzy and crazy, but it was fine. We had a good time. He can actually draw pretty well. Me, on the other hand, not the best."

She laughs. "Anyway, after that, we stopped by Sundae Scoop to grab some ice cream."

I nod along, pretending I'm interested. "Sounds like fun."

She looks up and smiles at me. "It was."

"So you got to know him a little better?"

She tilts her head from side to side. "Kinda. He doesn't talk about himself much. It's like pulling teeth to get him to say anything deep."

I bet.

"Yeah, I'm not sure I know much about him either," I say, turning into another town gossip. But I need information.

"Really? So it's not just me?"

I shake my head. "Nope. I hear different stories. I'm not sure where he's from or what his family is like. People say he's told them different things, so maybe he just had a bad childhood and has disassociated from it."

She leans forward, brows furrowing. "That's interesting because I knew someone who met him before and she said the same thing. He said he was from one place and then the next time they spoke, he said another place. He covered it up by saying he had lived in both, but it's kinda strange."

"So, he never brought up his family or anything like that with you?"

She sighs. "I asked a lot of questions, but he'd make a joke or skirt around it. All I got was that he has one sibling —a younger brother. He said he talks to his parents maybe once a month. I kinda sensed some bad blood."

Different from the details he told me.

I don't want to come off too inquisitive. She doesn't need to know why I'm so curious, but maybe if she sees him again, she can ask more questions. Perhaps I can learn through her, even if he's feeding her partial bullshit. Sometimes the truth slips out in small details.

I sigh. "Well, it's probably not a big deal."

"You're right."

"I'll talk to you later."

"Of course," she chirps.

AT LUNCH, I step outside and have a smoke. It's cold and snow has started to fall. It'll actually start accumulating by the end of the month, or for sure by early December. I pull my hood over my head and inhale another lungful of what'll surely kill me earlier than I'd like, but I can't stop. It's a habit, like many that I have, that I can't seem to break.

"Hey, you want something from Tino's?" Mark asks as he leaves.

"Get an extra-large of whatever you were planning on getting. I'll give you money when you get back."

"Cool."

Mark gets in his truck and heads to the pizza parlor, but as he's backing out, I glimpse a figure across the street. By the time Mark's pulled away, it's gone, but I know who it was. Kaspian is watching me again.

I continue to stare in the direction he was in, blowing smoke into the air. He's probably inside the flower shop since it has reflective windows. I can't see in, but he can see me.

After I put out my cigarette and drop the butt in the metal trash can, I pull out my phone and send him a message.

. . .

ME: *I know you're watching me.*

IT DOESN'T TAKE LONG for him to reply.

KASPIAN: *What are you talking about?*

I DON'T BOTHER RESPONDING, choosing instead to walk back inside where it's warm. Willow's on the phone when I pass her desk and head to the bathroom to wash my hands. When I make my way back to the front, I come to a stop when I see Kaspian in the lobby holding a small bouquet of flowers.

He grins at me.

Willow hangs up the phone and stands, rounding the desk. "Oh my gosh, are these for me?"

Kaspian hands them over. "Of course. I had fun last night."

Willow leans over the flowers to inhale their scent. "Me too. Let me see if I can find something in the breakroom to put these in. Be right back."

She rushes past me and into the back, leaving me alone with Kas.

"So, you weren't watching me. You were watching her," I say.

"Jealous?" he asks with a smirk.

"No. Curious."

He cocks his head. "Curious about what?"

"Your motives."

Because yesterday, after I found his little box of secrets,

it's become clear Kaspian seems to have ulterior motives. He's even more untrustworthy now.

"Motives?" he muses, brows furrowed, playing dumb. "I don't know what you mean."

I chance a glance behind me to make sure nobody's coming. "What do you want with Willow?"

"Why does it matter?"

"It only matters if you're going to do something that risks us getting caught."

Kaspian moves closer, lowering his voice to a whisper. "I'm not as stupid as you may think."

"I never said you were."

His eyes travel the length of my body and it stirs something in me. He sinks his teeth into his lower lip and meets my gaze again. His eyes are full of lust. "I want to fuck you."

I wasn't expecting those words, and my heart thumps in my chest. "That's nice," I say, downplaying how that statement made me feel. "I want to know what you're up to."

"Why do you think I'm up to anything?"

I level him with a look. "Aren't you always?"

He gives me a mischievous smile. "You didn't text me back yesterday."

"So you show up with flowers for my co-worker today?"

"Do you want some, too?" I ignore him and he steps even closer, his body almost touching mine. "No," he whispers, mouth hovering near my ear. "I know the types of gifts you like. Do you need me to round another one up?"

"I don't *need* anything from you."

He steps back, studying me, his face etched with anger. "Don't say that," he says through gritted teeth. "Because you know it's bullshit. You do need me, even if you don't know why yet. You fucking need me, Quintin."

My spine stiffens at the use of my name out in public. I narrow my eyes at him. "Why did you ask Willow out?"

His frustration morphs into a confusion. "What? She asked *me* out."

"It's not really a vase, but it'll work," Willow says, coming from the back with a tall, plastic Tupperware dish filled with flowers. "At least until I get home. Fucking Chad wouldn't let me use one of the many pots we have around here unless I pay for it."

We both look at her as she places them on her desk. I glance back at Kaspian. His confusion seemed real, but I'm not sure what the hell is *really* real about this guy.

I did some more research on him after I left his house Saturday night. His name brings nothing up anywhere, which leads me to believe it's not his birth name.

The picture I found makes the hair on the back of my neck stand up when I think about it. I could look into this further. I could maybe find out a little more information, but it requires doing what I've told myself I'd never do.

Someone clearing their throat drags me out of my thoughts. It's Kaspian. He's watching me with curiosity.

He knows who I am. He knows more about me than I thought I did. More than I've told him. It's only fair that I know more about him too. I have to do it. I have to know who I'm up against.

KASPIAN

TWENTY-THREE

S omething's wrong. Different. I can feel it.

Ezra's always had a cool detachment. His wariness around me was something I understood because I never know what to expect from him either.

But now, there's something else. He looks at me with even more distrust. His confusion is back. Before, it seemed as if he had gotten over the curiosity of why I am the way I am. I figured he came to terms with the fact that some people are messed up.

There's no way he could've figured out what brought me to him, and if he did, he would've said something, right?

No. He's too calculated for that.

I'll have to worry about that later. Right now, I have to focus on this Willow situation.

After I gave her the flowers and talked for a few minutes, I went back to work and started to do some plotting.

I GO the whole week without hearing from Ezra, which isn't too surprising. I'm usually the one who has to reach out first. However, I haven't done that. While I worry he may be at home planning my murder, I have more pressing issues to be concerned about.

Twice this week, I see Willow. On Wednesday, she showed up to my job to upgrade her phone. On Thursday evening, I ran into her at the grocery store. She was picking up wine and popcorn for a thrilling movie night with friends planned for Friday evening. I know that was the truth, because I watched the friends show up to her house that night.

Saturday, I knock on Ezra's door.

"Morning, sunshine," I greet.

He doesn't look amused. "It's two-thirty in the afternoon."

I shrug and blow hot air into my hands. "Kinda cold out here."

He rolls his eyes but steps back and lets me inside.

"What do you want, Kaspian?"

"I can't just stop by for a little afternoon delight?" I say with a grin, dropping to his couch. "It's been a while."

He comes around to sit in the armchair to my left. He's wearing light blue jeans and a white T-shirt, looking like he stepped out of an Old Navy ad. I can't help but laugh at the wholesome image.

"What's so funny?"

"Nothing. You look good."

"Right. So, what do you want?"

I sigh. "Can't just talk, can you?"

He leans forward. "Oh, sure. You wanna talk? Because I have plenty of questions."

I run my thumb along my jaw. "Oh yeah?"

"You can't start obsessing over Willow. She's too close to me, and not in an *I-have-feelings-for-her* type of way. I mean, if you start wanting to follow her around and get her to fall for your bullshit charm and lopsided smiles, just to get mad at her and kill her, we're going to have a problem. Police will question everyone at my job. They'll question me more because I've been seen out with her. I cannot have the cops looking into me. You understand? If you keep doing this shit, you're going to make me do something you don't want me to do."

My lips turn up on one side. "You like my lopsided smiles, don't you?"

"I'm fucking serious, Kaspian."

I exhale and stretch my legs out in front of me, crossing them at the ankles and draping an arm over the back of the couch. "Why do you think I'm following her?"

"It's what you do."

I lift a shoulder. "I suppose you're right but hear me out. Your friend Willow is following *me*."

He scoffs, sitting back in his chair. "You're delusional."

"I'm serious. She shows up where I am, not the other way around."

"Why would she be following you? Think she wants your dick that bad?"

I put my hand on my crotch. "It's pretty fucking good. Want a taste?"

His eyes drop to my lap, watching my hand move as I drag my palm across my shaft. He definitely wants it.

"You said she asked you out."

Well, guess I'm not getting a blow job right now. "Yeah."

"She told me you asked her out."

I shake my head. "I don't know why she'd say that."

"You realize I don't find you trustworthy at all, and

therefore have a hard time believing what you're saying is actually the truth."

"Fair, but I don't know how to prove it."

"Maybe it's just coincidences. I run into my neighbor fairly often, but it's because it's a small town," he says.

I shake my head. "Nah. This is different."

"Sure," he says with a sigh.

"You have any more questions?"

"Plenty. Why?"

I stand up. "Because I'm about to have your dick in my mouth and won't be able to answer them." I take a few steps to get to him and drop to my knees between his legs. "What are your questions?" I ask, reaching for the button of his jeans.

"What's your real name because I know it isn't Kaspian."

I pull the zipper down. "Kaspian is legally my name now."

He lifts his hips to allow me to pull the material down.

"Where are you from? And don't say Maine or Massachusetts or anything else with an M."

I reach into the slit in his boxer-briefs and wrap my fingers around his cock. "Texas."

"That's a lie."

"Florida."

He puts his hand in my hair, pulling the strands taut. "Stop fucking lying."

I lick my lips while I stare into his eyes and start stroking his cock. "Why do you want to know?"

His attempt to stay focused on his questions is threatened with every upstroke of his dick. I swirl my fist around his head, teasing the sensitive glans.

"Answer this, then," he rasps, loosening his grip on my

hair. "You said you saw me around town." He moans when I give his cock a squeeze at the base. "Said something about me drew you in, and that's why you started looking into me."

"Mm," I moan, drawing my fist up his shaft to see a drop of pre-cum emerge from the slit.

"That wasn't true, though. You already knew who I was, didn't you?"

I pause my movements and look up at him. "Yes. I already knew you."

Before he can open his mouth to ask more questions, I slide his cock across my tongue until it touches the back of my throat.

I worship his dick with my tongue, lips, and hands. I have him grunting and cussing, and I almost think I've gotten him to forget his line of questioning.

He moves to stand up, making me do the same. "Come here."

I follow him as he makes his way upstairs. We enter his bedroom but he quickly heads for another door. "Lube is in the drawer. Prep yourself before I get back unless you want it to hurt."

He closes himself in the bathroom while I do what he says. Naked and under his covers, I stretch my hole with my fingers, dying to feel him inside me again. He's gone for several minutes, and just when I'm starting to wonder if it was a door to another dimension instead of the bathroom, he returns.

"I was kinda hoping you'd be naked," I say, noticing he put on a pair of sweats while he was in there.

"Soon."

He yanks the covers back to reveal my naked body, his

nostrils flaring at the sight, and then he straddles me, taking my hands in his.

Transferring both my wrists to one hand, he uses his other to reach behind him and massage my balls as he grinds against my dick. He dry humps me for several seconds before his hand comes back up, pausing at his pocket to procure a pair of handcuffs that he promptly secures around my left wrist.

"What the fuck?"

He fastens the other end to the wooden post that stretches across his headboard before getting off me. Standing at the side of the bed, he digs into his pocket and produces a small pocketknife before stripping naked.

"Planning on torturing me?"

"If that's what it takes," he says as he crawls between my legs. "Do I need to secure your other hand or are you going to be a good boy?"

"Mm. I like that. Say it again."

He grabs the lube and squirts some on his cock, taking it in his hand and stroking his dick. He teases me by pushing his tip into my ass without breaching the rim.

"You want me to fuck you?"

"You know I do."

He pushes in a little more, pulling a hiss from my lips. "How much do you want me?"

He pulls out and I groan. "So fucking much."

"Mm," he moans, sliding all the way in, just to take it out again. "How did you know me, *Kaspian?*" He says my name mockingly.

"Please fuck me and I'll tell you whatever you want."

He chuckles deeply. "Not the way the game's played, I'm afraid."

"I thought you didn't play games."

His grin is smug. "I do when I make the rules."

Grabbing for the pocketknife, he pulls out a small blade. He dips his cock into my ass one more time before scooting back.

"Jesus," I breathe, closing my eyes.

The bed shifts and then I feel a warm, wet sensation drag across my shaft. My eyes fly open to find his tongue retreating into his mouth.

"Mm," he moans, licking his lips.

"Oh god. Please keep going."

He brings the blade to my chest, right next to my healed wound. He slices into me, making me buck. My free hand reaches out to grab his waist, my fingernails digging into his skin.

"Tell me," he says, eyes focused on his task. "Because I know you've been lying to me."

I slam my head deeper into his soft pillow, eyes squeezed close as I endure the burning sensation drag across my skin. When he stops, I take a deep breath and look into his eyes.

"You done now?"

"Nope."

He grabs my cock with his free hand and strokes, making sure I stay hard through the pain he's inflicting.

I do my best to ignore the throbbing in my chest and focus instead on his hand moving up and down my shaft.

"Yeah," I say with a moan.

He releases me instantly, leaning over my torso and bringing his mouth an inch from mine. "Tell me."

"Fuck me."

His lips quirk and he reaches down and positions his head at my hole, pushing in just enough that his crown disappears inside me.

"I don't know what you're planning, Kaspian, but remember this." He thrusts all the way in, ripping a cry from my throat. "I won't let you ruin my life." Thrust. "I won't let you kill me."

He pulls out and brings the blade back to my bloody, ruined chest.

"I don't know what you're talking about," I gasp. "Don't you realize..." I trail off as the blade penetrates my skin and drags down in a straight line. "Fuck."

"Don't I realize what?" he asks calmly, moving the blade over to do another cut.

"Don't you realize you're exactly what I want? Why would I do anything to remove you from my life?"

His eyes move to mine, studying me. "I wish I could believe you."

"Quintin, think about it. We're both fucked up. We know things about each other that nobody could ever know. You don't trust me and I think you'd kill me without giving it a second thought, but you know what? You'd miss me. You'd be bored without me. You need my type of craziness to make your life a little more interesting. We aren't normal by any means, but we're meant for each other. Tell me why I'd kill you."

He continues to stare at me for a few seconds before he finishes his work on my chest. His fingers run over the cuts, spreading the blood on my skin. His eyes darken and he drags his bloodied hand up to my neck, squeezing my throat as he shifts and shoves his cock back into my ass.

"Because I killed your dad. That's why."

A small, quiet noise escapes my mouth before his grip tightens on my throat.

EZRA

TWENTY-FOUR

His eyes bulge as he stares up at me, confusion etched across his handsome features. Not that he's confused by my statement, but at how I found out about it.

"Don't bullshit me anymore, Kas," I say, thrusting into him and sending his eyes rolling to the back of his head.

I release his throat and hitch his leg over my hip, pushing deep into his ass.

"I...how...it's..." He stumbles through his words. "Shit."

"That's right, baby. Figure out what lie you want to spew next."

"Oh god," he moans, his free hand gripping my thigh.

"You want revenge? Is that what this is about?"

"No!" he cries when I forcefully thrust into him.

I pull out and flip him over; he has to adjust his hand on the headboard before I take his hips in my hands and slide into him again.

"Why did you find me then? If not to turn me in or exact your revenge? Fucking tell me!" I roar, fucking him hard and fast.

He's nothing but grunts and moans, his free hand jacking his cock with fervor.

"You can't get rid of me, Kaspian."

"I don't want to."

My hips rock back and forth, my cock filling him up and stretching him wide. His pleasure filled noises crowd the room along with the sound of our bodies clashing together. My orgasm hits hard, my release exploding out of me and into his ass.

"Fuck!" I roar, holding him tight as my body vibrates with the aftershocks.

"Oh my god," he cries, his forehead pressing into the headboard as he comes on my pillow.

I grab the knife and wrap my arm around his chest, hand pressing against his fresh wounds as I yank him up as much as I can. My chest collides into his back and I bring the blade to his throat.

With my mouth at his ear, I say, "Give me one reason not to slit your throat right fucking now."

He sucks in deep breaths for a handful of seconds. "If I go missing, your secret will no longer be safe." He pauses. "You need me alive. I have other photos. I have your name written down."

I stay there at his back, blade pressed to his flesh as I contemplate what I want to do. Part of me wants to let the knife slide across his throat, but the other part of me knows I shouldn't do something without a fool-proof plan. Eventually, I pull away from him and unlock the handcuffs before I walk around the bed and grab my clothes. "Get the fuck out of my house."

He turns around, his chest bloody. "I think we should talk."

"Oh, we will," I seethe. "But not today. If I hear

anything else come out of your mouth right now, I may kill you regardless of the consequences."

He moves to gather his clothes, his actions slow since I've destroyed both his ass and chest. "I couldn't tell you that I knew, Quintin. How would that have gone? *Hey, I know you killed my dad, but let's hang out.*"

I glare at him as I pull my pants on. "Why the fuck would you befriend the man who killed your dad? I know you're fucked up, but to fuck your father's killer? You have a motive. I know you well enough to know that."

"You don't know half of what there is to know about me, but let me know when you're ready to actually listen. Not just cut and fuck me." He steps into his pants and instead of attempting to put on his shirt, he just drapes it over his shoulder so the material covers the wounds. "But remember, as much as you love doing those things, I love being on the receiving end. I won't allow you or anybody else to ruin this for us."

TWENTY-FIVE

"Fucking crazy ass," I mutter to myself after Kaspian leaves.

I jump in the shower before stripping my bed bare and throwing everything in the washing machine. Kaspian's good at spewing bullshit and saying things he thinks people want to hear, so it's hard to trust his word. However, considering his attachment to me, and the fact that he's yet to try to hurt me, let alone kill me, I'm inclined to believe it's not his intention. But that doesn't mean he doesn't have one. Maybe he's trying to get me to let my guard down around him so he can strike.

When I determined it was time to look into my past crimes, I found out a little more about Kaspian, namely that he's not Kaspian at all. Which I figured. In fact, his name is Jasper Castillo. Jasper is the son of Salvador Castillo—an undercover cop found murdered in an abandoned house. My reason for fleeing the state of Washington.

I've never looked into the murders I've committed. Sure, they were on the news for a little while, because serial killers always get airtime, but Salvador's death wasn't staged to look like he was killed by the Heart Stopper. Being an officer got him plenty of attention, though. Too much for my liking. I left and vowed to never look into his case.

As soon as I saw the photo of him in Kaspian's locked box, I knew it was only a matter of time until I had to. I didn't remember ever seeing news about him having a son in the days after he was found; the wife was talked about, though.

I recently found out that Jasper was the product of Salvador's first marriage. The woman at his funeral was his second wife and they didn't have kids together.

There's more to this story that I need to hear, but it's a little unnerving to realize that the kill that had me spooked enough to flee the state is coming back around. His death was never solved. Justice never received. And his son is a vengeful sociopath.

WEEKS GO by without speaking to Kaspian. I see him, though. He's everywhere. He comes to my job and talks to Willow. He drinks his coffee a few tables away in The Perfect Blend, watching me over every sip. He's shown up to Thai Me Down while I've had dinner, but he never speaks. He's waiting for me to make the first move.

I've debated what I want to do, even contemplating moving again and starting over. I was doing pretty good until I came across Kaspian. I could do it again. I looked up towns in Iowa and Nebraska, but the idea of being in another shitty, small town that offers nothing exciting makes me want to kill myself instead of anybody else. Maybe Chicago or Houston would be better, but the idea of not having Kaspian around is what gives me pause. He was right, I do need him, but not for the reason he thinks. He believes I need him alive because I risk the chance of being found out if he goes missing, but the real reason is because even though I'm not good at showing it, I like his presence. Even if we're not physically together, I know he's out there, lurking in the shadows, obsessing over why I haven't texted him and hating every man I talk to.

The sex is the best I've ever had, with a man or a woman. I don't have to hold back. I choke him and his cock hardens. I cut him, and though it hurts, he never begs me to stop. He needs the pain like I need to inflict it.

I'll never find another person like him again. I know that, and so does he. I guess it's time to hear him out.

"I feel like we haven't hung out in a while," Willow says, coming up next to me as I'm getting ready to leave work.

"Yeah. I've just had a lot going on."

She tilts her head and puts her hand on my shoulder. "Everything okay? Is it your dad?"

"What?" I ask, and then I remember the lie I told back in October. "Oh. No. Just some other stuff."

"Well, if you feel like getting out of your head a little, me, Jason, Cora, Sam, BJ, and Kaspian are all going to be at The Hideout tonight. Your first drink is on me."

She grins, but I can't help but focus on one name. "Kaspian?"

"He's been hanging out with us the last couple weekends."

I nod my head. "Cool. Maybe I'll show up."

Her smile grows. "Good. I hope so." She fidgets, shifting her weight as she wrings her hands in front of her.

"You okay?"

"Yeah. Umm." She contemplates saying something else,

but then she just laughs. "Never mind. I'll talk to you later. If you come out."

I nod. "Okay."

She scurries off, and I wonder if she and Kaspian have gone out on any more dates. She doesn't bring him up often, and any idea of a threesome seems to have died. I'm not sure I'd even want to do that with those two. I like being with Kaspian the way we've been, and to add someone to the mix would be to water it down.

I drive home and debate on showing up. On one hand, I hate clubs and people and having to pretend I'm enjoying myself when I'd rather be at my house, but on the other hand, Kaspian will be there, and I wonder if he'll actually speak words to me.

I SHOW UP LATE, wanting to minimize my time in the club. The group has pulled two tables together and while half of them are in the seats, the others are standing around, half dancing and half drinking. Mostly empty glasses litter the tables along with soaked napkins that seem to have been used to clean a spill.

My eyes find Kaspian in the chair at the end, his left leg stretched out while his other leg remains under the table. He's slouched comfortably in the wooden chair, his arm slung around the back of the one next to him. The one that Willow sits in.

His dark eyes are on me, a slight smirk tugging on his lips. My cock twitches just from looking at him. His hair is cut short on the sides, rocking a new fade that leads to spiky textured pieces of hair up top.

Willow turns and spots me, her eyes growing in size as she leaps up and runs to give me a hug.

"You made it!"

I wrap my arms around her, my eyes never leaving Kaspian's. "I did. Sorry I'm late."

"Better late than never," Kas says from his seat.

"Want a drink?" Willow asks.

"I'll grab one."

"But I told you I'd buy your first one. Don't make me a liar. Tell me what you want and I'll go get it."

"Just a beer is fine."

"Type?"

"Buyer's choice," I say with a wink.

Once she's gone, I take a few steps to get to the table and say hi to Jason and Samantha who are sitting on the other end before I pull out the chair across from Kaspian and sit down.

We stay locked on each other for a while before he speaks. "Glad to see you haven't left town yet."

I cock a brow at him. "Why would I leave?"

"You tell me. You're the one looking up places in, what was it? Iowa?"

I run the pad of my thumb across the side of my chin as I lean in. "And how would you know that, Jasper?"

His nostrils flare as he clenches his jaw. "You think I just fixed your phone when you brought it to me? I know everything you do because of that phone."

I shake my head. "Of fucking course."

He grins and holds his arms out to the side. "Come on. Are you really surprised?"

"I suppose not."

He reaches up and adjusts the small hoop on his nose. "I

193

guess you've been looking me up on your computer because I didn't see that."

I nod. "Jasper Castillo. Nice name."

"Don't say that name again," he says, his lips barely moving.

"That's your name, though." I glance around to make sure everyone is still preoccupied. "The son of Salvador. A cop." I laugh. "I find that amusing."

"I'm glad you do."

"Why did Jasper become Kaspian? That's what I want to know."

"Is that the only thing you want to know?"

"No, but it's a start."

"Not the best place to talk," he says, turning his head toward the bar.

I follow his gaze and find Willow coming back with my drink.

"Here you go."

"Thanks."

For the next hour we put our conversation on hold, talking to Willow and Cora instead. Samantha and BJ spend a lot of time on the dance floor, while Jason does his best to act like he's not watching them. Eventually, Willow lures Kaspian and Cora to the bar to help her get a round of shots and a few more drinks.

Jason sits down next to me with a huff.

"What's up, man? You didn't tell her whatever you know about BJ?"

He sighs. "I did! I sent the message from a fake Instagram account, but she never replied after seeing it. If they fought about it, I can't tell. They seem happier than ever."

"That sucks. Maybe you should just forget about her. There's a ton of girls here."

"I know."

Kaspian appears, placing shot glasses in front of Jason and me. "What're y'all gossiping about?"

"BJ," Jason groans.

"Blow jobs?"

Jason laughs, already tipsy. "BJ. Sam's boyfriend."

Kaspian looks at me and I jerk my head toward the love-birds on the dance floor.

"Oh, that douchebag? I hate that guy."

"Why?" Jason asks.

Kas shrugs. "Just a weird vibe I get."

"Jason's in love with Samantha, but she's with BJ," I say.

Jason elbows me, chuckling. "I'm not *in love*."

"Want me to kill him?" Kas asks. "Me and Ez can get rid of him for you."

Luckily, Jason thinks it's a joke and starts laughing. "I wish. He's such a dick."

The three of us take our shots and then the girls get back and whine that we didn't wait for them. After another thirty minutes, five of which have consisted of Kaspian rubbing his leg against mine under the table, I get up and go to the bathroom.

When I return to the table, it's just to tell them I'm going to go outside for a smoke. It doesn't take long for someone to follow me out, but it's not Kaspian like I expected.

"Hey," Willow says sheepishly, crossing her arms in front of her as she attempts to stay warm. She put on her coat, but it looks like it's made more for fashion than warmth.

"Hey." I blow smoke away from her.

"This may be weird but I just wanted to ask you a question."

"Okay," I say, taking another drag.

"How good of friends are you with Kaspian?"

My brows pull together. She's asked a variation of this before. "What are you asking exactly?"

She looks off to the side. "Sometimes I feel like you guys barely know each other and other times I feel like you have a stronger connection."

I wonder if everyone sees what she does. Is it obvious there's more between us? And does she even have the right to know? Plus, what Kaspian and I are is hard to explain. Hardly dating and in love. Not exactly best friends. What she said explains it perfectly. There are times where I don't think I know him at all, yet I feel like he's the only person in the world who gets me.

Bringing the butt of the cigarette to my lips, I inhale slowly, staring down at her while I wonder what it is she's wanting to hear. Or maybe what she doesn't.

The door to the bar opens, letting music and loud chatter penetrate the relative silence outside.

"Well, I don't know about you guys, but I think I'm done for the night," Kaspian says, his hands coming to rest on my shoulders as he gives me a squeeze before moving toward Willow to give her a hug. "Thanks for inviting me out. Are we still on for lunch on Wednesday?"

Her lips twitch slightly as her eyes narrow briefly. She looks tense, her eyes flickering to me for half a second before she focuses on Kaspian and smiles. "Yes, of course."

She doesn't want me to know they're...dating? Is that why she's asking about me and him? Is she jealous? Or does she think I'll be upset that she moved on from having interest in me to going out with him?

"Okay, cool," Kas responds before turning to walk away from us.

I put my cigarette out on the brick building behind me and toss it in the trash. "I think I'm going to call it a night, too," I announce, glancing at my watch.

"Oh. Okay."

"Have a good night, Willow."

I walk in the opposite direction Kaspian went, pulling my hood over my head to protect me from the biting wind. I make it around the corner and look up to find Kas leaning against the side of my truck.

"Ready to talk?"

TWENTY-SIX

Not wanting to take him back to my house, I drive us to an overlook with a view of a pond surrounded by countless trees. However, it's late, and you can't see much, but we're not here to take pictures. It's quiet and secluded, allowing us the privacy we need for the talk we're about to have.

"All right. Talk."

Kas unbuckles his seatbelt and shifts in the seat to face me. "What do you want to know?"

"Everything. From the beginning."

He sighs, running a hand through his hair. "My dad left my mom and me when I was eleven. He had never been a good father or husband. He was absent a lot, and when he was around, he was angry. He hated us. There's no other way to explain it. He beat my mom first, and then he started hitting me."

I nod my head a couple times, realizing why and when his issues started to form. "An alcoholic?"

"He drank, but it's not like he was abusive because he was an alcoholic. He was abusive because he was a terrible person." He exhales, rubbing his palm over his forehead a few times as he stares at the dashboard. "Anyway, he did... other things. To me. Probably to her. He was never one that felt he needed permission to do anything."

His eyes find mine briefly, his head still down, and it's the first time he's shown any sort of insecurity. He doesn't have to say anything else for me to understand what he's talking about. My anger bubbles inside me.

"When he left, it was a relief, even if we struggled. Not having hot water or food every day was easy to live with when you didn't have to worry about being abused. But, when I was thirteen, my mom disappeared and I had to stay with my dad again. Everything picked up like it never ended. My mom didn't pop back up for another two years, and as mad as I was at her for leaving me in the first place, I jumped at the chance of moving back in with her and her new husband. She said she left to get her life together. She claimed to have gone to rehab and therapy and that's where she found her new guy, Craig. By that time, I was fifteen, and the damage had already been done.

"My formative years were fucked. I had trust issues and abandonment issues. I was a victim nearly my whole life and I was tired of it. After a year, Craig couldn't handle me. I was the cause of many arguments between him and my mom. I didn't listen to him and he tried disciplining me, but I wouldn't let that happen. We had several fights that ended in broken dishes and furniture. Mom tried making it work for another year before she couldn't anymore. She chose him, and once again I was left behind. I refused to live with my dad. I didn't even tell him she left. We hadn't spoken in years anyway.

"I went about my life, working and couch surfing, saving money for the cheapest place I could rent. One day, when I was almost twenty, I ran into my dad again. He was with his new wife, and when I stopped in front of them, he didn't introduce me as his son. He stumbled his way through some bullshit lie and hurried away before I could spill the beans. He never told her about me and it made me snap. It was all I thought about for months. I was planning on killing him myself, but you got to him first."

His eyes slowly lift to mine. "Were you there?" I ask.

"I was nearby. I had been following him and knew where he was working. I saw you talk to him but didn't think much of it. Not until he left with you and never returned. Hours went by as I sat in my car down the road, and eventually you emerged, but he never did. I followed you back to your place just so I knew where to find you, and then I went back and found him."

"What'd you do?"

He scoffs. "What could I do? I stared down at his body and all I could feel was rage. I wanted to be the one to kill him. I *deserved* to be the one to kill him!" he spits, his voice rising with his anger. "You took that from me."

"I regret not making it hurt worse," I tell him honestly.

Kas exhales through his nose. "I couldn't stay long, but when I left, I went back to your house, looked in the mailbox to find out your name, and then dug up everything I could."

"So everything you said before about finding out about me was a lie."

He shrugs. "Maybe. But I became obsessed with finding out who you were. Not just your name, but what made you want to kill him. I wondered if you had the same history with him as I did somehow. But then I found out about your parents, and nothing made sense. You had no ties to my dad. Your parents were killed by a budding serial killer, but because I knew what you did to my dad, I questioned that. I looked into the other victims of the serial killer and came to the conclusion that you were just some twisted fuck who got off on killing people."

"I do it because it releases something in me. I feel better and calmer afterward."

He shrugs. "You don't have to explain it to me. I'm well aware."

I chew on my bottom lip as I study him. "Did you follow me here?"

"Obviously."

"I mean even as I traveled through other states?"

He shakes his head. "I put a tracker on your truck while you were still in Washington. I watched from a distance."

I shake my head. "I can't believe you."

"I told you not to underestimate me." He grins, happy with himself.

"Once I knew you were here to stay, I took my time. I had to save money so I could make the move across country. It took a little while, but then, my relationship ended and I thought it was the best time to move."

"Ended with death?"

He smirks. "Mm."

"So you got here and started stalking women."

"I wouldn't call it that. I was just getting your attention."

"That you did."

His lips stretch across his face again before the smile drops. "I'm still pissed that you killed my dad before I could."

"I can't say I regret doing it, especially now."

He ducks his head. "Don't pity me."

"I don't pity anyone."

201

"I can believe that."

"So, you don't want to kill me for killing your dad, and you don't want to kill me because I took the opportunity from you, so what do you want?"

He takes a breath, eyes meeting mine from across the cab of the truck. "In the beginning, I just wanted to understand you. I was fascinated. You had done what I contemplated for a long time and didn't seem to struggle with it."

"I contemplated plenty of things for many years. I was just born this way. I don't have stories of trauma, but eventually everything that was inside me came to a head. When I did it, I expected to feel something. I figured I'd be overcome with guilt and grief, but I never felt anything but relief."

"I struggled my first time. Panicked. Became paranoid. Once I realized nobody was suspecting me of anything, I started to calm down. I learned to be a little smarter, but I'm still quick to anger. It's hard to think rationally sometimes."

"Sometimes," I say with a chuckle.

"Oh, fuck off."

"In the beginning you said you wanted to understand me. What about now?"

He stares at me, contemplating his answer, probably debating on the truth versus what he thinks I want to hear.

"Honestly, I thought I wanted to kill you. If I couldn't kill him, maybe murdering his killer would be good enough." He takes a breath. "But then it started to feel like I'd be doing something *for* him, and he doesn't deserve shit. He's not entitled to justice or vengeance. He got exactly what he deserved, but part of me will always regret not taking action sooner." He pauses. "What made you kill your parents?"

I shake my head. "It's hard to explain, but I think I always had something wrong with me. I was never a happy kid. Chronically upset, without a reason I could explain. My parents were decent enough, but absent. They knew something was wrong with me, I think, and they didn't know how to deal with me. I overheard conversations, but the breaking point was when I had finally learned to blend in with societal norms. In their eyes, they should've seen a happier person, capable of normal emotions. I was perfecting it. They found me even more odd. They talked about me and stayed away from me. Even after all I had done in an effort to make them like me. So —" I shrug.

"They had to go," Kas finishes.

"Basically. I felt better after. It was no longer necessary to put on a front. Not that it seemed to do any good anyway." Kas nods, and I continue. "So, again, what do you want from me now?"

His dark eyes meet mine, and he stares at me for several long seconds before he answers. "I just want you to want me the way I want you."

"And how's that?"

"Overwhelmingly and all-consuming. I want you to feel my absence like you'd feel a knife in your chest. I don't need you to tell me you love me. I'm not sure I'd believe it anyway. Love feels obligatory in a relationship. Like you have to say it even if you don't mean it. Love is just a trite four-letter word. People use it for every fucking thing. They love a movie, a song, a particular cup of coffee. I don't want to be lumped into a bunch of random shit. What I want is to be accepted and desired. I want to be craved. I want you to feel like you'd be miserable without me."

He stares back at me, waiting for my response. I

unbuckle my seatbelt and slide out from under the wheel across the bench seat. His eyes track my movements.

I point at his chest. "Did you see my little gift to you?"

His fingers brush gently across his shirt, right where my cuts were inflicted. "I did."

"I took a knife to your chest and carved my name into your skin. My real name. Tell me that doesn't mean something."

His teeth drag across his bottom lip. "Means you want to brand me."

"It means you're mine."

"Yours," he says softly. "You did it right after you found out about my dad. You almost killed me that day. Your confession was basically scribbled across my chest."

"If I had killed you, I'd have cut that from your skin."

"Always thinking a step ahead," he says with a small grin.

"Look, I won't tell you I love you, but I'll always tell you I want you."

Kaspian smiles slowly. "Yeah?"

"Yeah, and right now, I want you naked and on my dick."

KASPIAN

CHAPTER TWENTY-SEVEN

S tripped of our clothes and prepped, thanks to a packet of lube I shoved in my pocket for moments just like these, I bounce up and down on Quintin's cock.

His hands run up my sides and around my back before lowering to my ass where he squeezes my cheeks. I have one arm slung around his neck with the other one braced against the back window, my head bent and nuzzled into his neck so I don't keep banging it on the roof.

"Fuck, you feel so good," I breathe.

"You feel how much I want you?" he grunts, moving his hands to my hips and lifting his own to push deeper inside me. "Every inch of my desire for you?"

"Yes, I fucking feel it," I moan.

"Good."

I sit back, putting space between our chests, and he brings his hand to his mouth and spits in his palm before wrapping his fingers around my shaft.

"Yes, oh god."

He strokes slowly at first, teasing me with his grip. I

grind back and forth and open my eyes to find him watching me. He nearly takes my breath away with the unbridled lust in his gaze.

"You said you wouldn't look at me like that," I whisper huskily.

"Like what?"

"Like I was the prettiest thing you've ever seen."

"You're not," he breathes, stroking faster. "Pretty isn't a word I'd use to describe you. You're volatile and arousing. You're captivating and dangerous." He moans when I rock into him. "You're absolutely devastating."

I close my eyes and drop my head back, soaking up his words. His hand picks up speed at the same time my hips do. His other hand comes to rest on the side of my neck, his thumb brushing over my Adam's apple.

"Quin." His name leaves my lips on a whisper. "Oh god."

He grips my face tightly. "Look at me."

My eyelids flutter open and meet his penetrating gaze. "I'm so close."

His lips are on mine in a flash, his tongue plundering my mouth. It's our first kiss, after all this time, and it's earth-shattering.

I never thought twice about the fact that he hadn't kissed me. He didn't come off as the type. I was happy enough to have his eyes on me when we were in the same room, to have his hands on me when we fucked. Even felt myself lucky to be on the other end of his blade because I knew he was capable of killing me, like many others, and yet never did. I didn't think I was missing out until now.

His kiss is possessive, but I fight for control. Our tongues dance together until I suck his into my mouth. He forces us even closer by placing his hand at the back of my head and not allowing me to escape the lashing of his tongue. He swallows my moans while I taste his desire.

This kiss isn't a regular kiss. It's not simply lips meeting lips and the soft brush of tongues. He's brutal and demanding, wanting to lick and taste every square inch of my mouth. His free hand roams my body, rubbing and squeezing. I thread my fingers in his hair before cupping his jaw and growling into his mouth. We devour each other for a long while, his hand still on my cock, though his movements paused during our kiss.

He pulls away, both of us breathing heavily as we stare at each other. That kiss was the most honest form of communication we've had.

"Give me your tongue," he commands.

I stick it out as far as it'll stretch and watch as he takes the tip between his lips and slowly sucks it into his mouth, repeating the movement the way I want him to do on my cock. He moans and it sends a jolt of electricity down my spine, energizing me. I rise and fall on his dick until my orgasm builds to a breaking point.

The noises I make are shameless. Quintin releases my tongue, his lips glistening with my saliva. "I want every last drop."

Another sinful moan leaves my throat. I've never felt so out of control with lust. I'm dying to come, but also want to live right here on the edge, where everything is heightened and sensitive.

"I don't want it to end," I admit.

"We're just getting started," he growls. "Now come for me. Paint my skin with your release."

"Oh shit!"

My orgasm hits hard, cum shooting from my cock and landing on his stomach.

"Oh yeah," he groans, watching me make a mess.

"Fuck," I pant. "Oh my god."

Once he's squeezed everything from me, he grabs my waist and lifts me up just to impale me on his cock. He does this over and over, hard and fast.

"Oh, fuck." He moans, his muscles flexing as he continues to control me. "Oh, god. Yeah." Cries of pleasure leave his lips as he shatters, his cock twitching inside me as he comes.

We suck in deep breaths, moaning and cursing as we continue to live in the euphoria of each other.

I WAKE up Sunday morning in Quin's bed and find myself alone. After taking a piss, I go through his bathroom drawers and find three unopened packages of toothbrushes stacked neatly. The cabinet under his sink is orderly, extra body wash and lotions in a neat row next to rolls of toilet paper and unused loofahs.

"Neat freak," I mutter, taking a toothbrush package and ripping it open.

After I've cleaned myself up, I open the door and find Quin sitting on the edge of the bed looking at his phone.

"I used one of your toothbrushes, but don't worry, you have extras."

He makes a slight noise but doesn't look up. He's wearing only his pajama bottoms, his light, golden brown skin flawless in the early morning light.

Wearing only my underwear, I make my way between his legs, running a hand through his hair. He looks up at me then, his face near my crotch.

I grin down at him. "Care to show my cock the same attention you showed my mouth last night?"

His hand skates up the back of my thigh, squeezing my ass cheek. "No, thank you."

I roll my eyes. "At least you were polite about it." Dropping to my knees, I place my hands on his muscled thighs, running them up to his hips. "Have you thought about me fucking you?"

He puts his phone down, leaning back on his palms. "Why do you ask?"

"Because I want to fuck you."

He scrutinizes me for a while before he replies. "It may have been a fleeting thought."

"Fleeting," I repeat, kneading his thighs. "Why?"

"I like being in control."

My fingers find their way to his waistband, tugging it down. "You don't trust me."

"I never said that."

"Do you?"

He lifts his ass off the bed so I can pull his pants down. "Should I?"

I have a feeling he's talking about more than just sex. I give him a one shouldered shrug. "Maybe."

"Convincing."

"You can top from the bottom," I say, planting a kiss on his inner thigh.

"Mmhmm," he moans, maintaining eye contact with me as I continue kissing a path up to his hip bone.

"I want to be inside you. You could ride me. Tie my hands to the headboard and bounce on my dick." I lick a path through his trimmed pubic hair.

His cock twitches and a groan rumbles in his throat. "It's just not something I've done."

"Ever?" I ask, my breath ghosting across his shaft before I swipe my tongue under his tip.

He moans. "No."

"Mm. I could be your first."

"Shut up and suck me."

I chuckle, but I don't listen to him. Instead, I move lower, letting my tongue drag down his erection until I reach his balls. I lick and suck them into my mouth before I reach his ass. I take hold of his thighs and spread his legs further apart, holding them up slightly so I can rim his hole.

He hisses, lying flat on his back. "Fuck."

"I'd make sure you were nice and ready," I whisper before swiping my tongue between his cheeks again. I push his legs up even higher, spreading him open for me. My tongue dips into his ass. "God, you taste so good."

Quintin moans and it spurs me on. I hold his cheeks apart and lick around his entrance before prodding at it with the tip of my tongue. Each time I penetrate, I try to put a little more inside.

"Jesus Christ."

"You like it?" I ask before another swipe of my tongue slides over his hole. "I could fucking taste you all day." I reach for his cock and find it leaking like a broken faucet. My hand slides over his sticky arousal. "Oh, you fucking love it."

"My god," he moans. "Come up here."

I tease him for a few more seconds before I get to my feet. Quintin scoots up onto the bed and I remove my boxer-briefs before laying over him, my cock heavy against his.

He takes my jaw in his hand, pulling my mouth closer to his before he swipes his tongue over my lips and chin, and then smashes his mouth against mine in a vicious kiss.

He licks his own taste from my tongue, and I grind against him.

I move my hips, letting my cock fall between his thighs and poke at this entrance. He tenses briefly.

"Just the tip?" I tease, pushing in closer to him.

"That's what they always say," he groans. "It's never just the tip."

"Who's they?" I ask, getting on my knees.

"Figure of speech. Shut up."

I take my dick in my hand and push his leg to the side, swiping my head up and down his taint. "God, you're so fucking perfect."

He wraps his fingers around his shaft, tugging on his cock as I tease his hole. I stick two fingers in my mouth and get them wet before I slide them between his cheeks and press.

"Oh fuck," he grunts, eyes snapping to mine.

I spit, letting it fall to where my digits meet his ass. His eyes close and I push in a fraction of an inch. I continue to tease him—tease *us*. We both stroke our dicks with slow movements while I play with his ass. I get the tip of one finger inside and then push his leg up and press the head of my cock to his entrance. I don't make a move to slide inside, but Quin moves closer, arching off the bed slightly.

"Mm."

Both of us moan at the same time. My cock is hard and throbbing in my hand, ready to explode. His drips to his abdomen, desperate for a release as well.

"Just the tip," he whispers roughly, hand moving faster on his shaft.

I quickly lower myself and lick his hole, spitting for more lubrication before I do the same in my palm to slather on my crown.

I'm sure he has lube in here somewhere, but I'm too impatient and desperate to stop and look for it. I spread his legs and ever so slowly begin to push my head into him. I watch as he starts to stretch around me, opening up and taking me in.

"Holy fuck," I exclaim.

Quin is quiet except a low grunt, his face strained and muscles flexed as he continues to stroke. His heat envelopes my head, and his tight ass threatens to suck me all the way in. I want nothing more than to dive deep and fuck him into the mattress, but...just the tip.

I want him to trust my word. I'm not the most reliable or trustworthy, but with this, I will be.

Once my crown is fully submerged, suffocating in his grip, I use my hand to stroke myself. My movements are slow and careful, but the image before me is enough to send me over the edge. The veins in his forearm protrude, his thick cock in hand. His body shifts enough to drive me crazy, and I watch as he clenches around me.

"Jesus, Quin. I'm gonna come."

His heavy breaths mix with lusty groans, and I feast on the sight before me as white streams of cum shoot from his tip, landing in the cuts of his abs. His body jerking around me sends a tingling sensation to my groin that has my balls tightening. Pleasure shoots through my cock and I pull out just in time to watch my own release exploding onto him, sending me into a world of ecstasy.

I collapse at his side, and we lay there for a few minutes before getting up to get cleaned. Our bubble of bliss pops when I emerge from the shower after he's already gotten out. I have only a towel wrapped around my waist and make my way downstairs to ask about borrowing a pair of underwear, but before I get to the bottom, I hear voices.

ISABEL LUCERO

"Ezra, I don't know what to do. I feel like I'm going crazy. I don't know what to think or believe, or if I can even trust myself. I'm...I'm just out of it, and I can't even tell anyone what I'm thinking. I feel like I'm losing my mind."

Willow.

She's blubbering like a child, her sobs breaking up her sentences.

"Whoa, whoa," he replies. "What are you talking about? What happened?"

Willow cries some more. "I don't know."

I peek around the corner, careful to stay hidden, and find him holding her in a hug as she weeps on his shoulder.

"It's gonna be okay," he offers. A promise he can't make.

"I just want to forget. Even if it's only for a little bit," she says right before she throws her arms around his neck and plants her lips on his.

214

TWENTY-EIGHT

I watch with confusion for just a second before Quintin gently grabs her by the shoulders and pushes her back. "Wait."

She wipes her cheek, looking at him with pain in her eyes. "I'm sorry. God, I feel so stupid."

"It's okay," he says patiently.

"Ezra," she says with a sniffle. "Do you think people can change who they are?"

The question feels like it came straight out of left field. The pause before he answers lets me know it catches him off guard.

"If they want to, they can. You can always become a better person if you want to change."

She shakes her head, eyes frantic and wild. "No, not like that. I mean...Ugh. I don't know. Never mind." Willow waves her hand in the air before taking a couple steps toward the door. She turns around and looks at him. "Do you think you're a good judge of character?"

"I'd like to think so," he replies.

She gives him a sad, pitiful smile. "Be careful, Ezra." And then she turns around and leaves.

I wait several seconds before I join him.

"What the fuck was that about?" I ask.

He looks over his shoulder at me. "I don't know."

Sauntering toward him, I say, "You know, I've come to find something out."

"What's that?" he asks, turning to face me fully.

Slipping my fingers into the waistband of his sweats, I tug him into me. "I'm no longer blasé about you being with a woman."

His lips pull up into a smirk. "Hmm."

"Mm," I moan, leaning closer. "I didn't appreciate seeing that kiss."

Quintin stares back at me, unflinching. "It didn't last long."

"Now that I've had a taste of your mouth, I don't want it on anyone else."

"So, lick the taste of her lips from mine."

I don't hesitate. My tongue darts out and dances softly across his bottom lip before dragging across the top one. I press a quick kiss to his mouth before I ease back.

"Better."

"Much." He studies me, eyes traveling down my naked torso. "Get some clothes on and let's eat."

"I could leave them off and you could still eat."

His eyes flare. "Later."

I grin. "Holding you to that. Can I wear something of yours?"

"Grab whatever you want," he says, turning to head to the kitchen.

216

UNFORTUNATELY, we only have time to eat actual food before I need him to take me back to my car so I can go to work, but when I get off seven hours later, I plan on going right back to him, whether he expects me to or not. I'm addicted to the way his tongue works, and we have so much more left to do.

Before I get into my car, something catches my eye across the parking lot. I study the darkened street where most stores are already closed. Through falling snowflakes and bristling wind, I think I make someone out. Someone who's caught my attention.

New plan.

I follow the figure as they move, unaware of the tail they've picked up. Their hood is up and pulled snug, covering both sides of their face in an effort to keep the wind from throwing cold snow across their cheeks. They keep their head down, peeking up enough to make sure they don't run into anybody or anything.

There aren't many people on the streets on a Sunday night, and the ones out right now are hurrying to their cars or buildings, not worried about anything but getting out of the cold.

The figure darts into Perfectly Convenient, but I stay outside, pulling my coat tight around me as I huddle on the side of the building across the street. They move through the store, grabbing a couple of items, but the hood remains on, as do the black gloves on their hands.

When they get to the register, they chat with the worker —a young redheaded woman. I can make out a bit of concern on her face as she listens to the customer before her eyes bounce around, looking for something. She gestures to someone else and a man takes over her spot while she walks away.

They disappear around the corner, and I can no longer see them through the glass doors. I contemplate getting closer, but I don't want to risk being seen. After about ten minutes, they both return to the front, but the customer never buys the items she had chosen.

She turns and heads for the door, her face visible under the bright fluorescent lights before she tucks her chin and steps into the cold.

Willow.

She was lurking outside my job before I came out. I told Quintin she had been following me, and this is just another instance. Is she obsessed with me? I've never had the tables turned on me like this. It's...interesting.

EZRA

TWENTY-NINE

Once again, Kaspian has disappeared. After our time together on Sunday, he went to work and never showed back up. A small part of me thought he would, but he's also prone to doing his own thing without a word.

On Wednesday, however, I expect to see him. Not because I think he'll come to see me, but because I remember him mentioning the day to Willow. They had a lunch date planned, and I'm starting to wonder what the hell is going on between them.

He's made it clear he doesn't want to see me with men or women. He's possessive and jealous, which I can understand, yet he's going out with Willow.

That's not to say they're fucking. Maybe they're just friends. But something about it seems weird to me, and I can't quite put my finger on it. They both seem to be forcing this to happen, but why?

We've not discussed what we are. Being a couple sounds weird, calling him my boyfriend is even stranger. Our relationship doesn't fit within the bounds of what's deemed an acceptable and normal relationship, so I don't think we should tarnish it with labels that don't fit. We are what we are—dysfunctional.

I'm sure to be in the lobby around the time Willow takes her lunch.

"Hey," she says sheepishly as I walk up to her desk. "I'm so embarrassed about showing up to your place. Please erase it from your memory."

"What are you talking about?" I ask with a small grin.

She looks up at me and gives me an appreciative smile. "You're the best."

Truth of the matter is, her words still linger in my brain. *I feel like I'm going crazy. I'm losing it. Do you think people can change who they are? Be safe.*

"How you doin', though?" I ask.

She sighs. "Oh, I'm fine." Her hands shake as she moves a folder to a drawer. She's far from fine.

In fact, she's slowly becoming a little more frazzled and distracted. I've noticed small changes in her the past couple weeks.

"You going out to lunch with Kaspian?"

She freezes briefly before her eyes meet mine. "Yeah. Do you want to come?"

I shake my head. "I wasn't looking for an invitation," I say with a chuckle.

"I mean, it's fine. It's not a big deal. We're not like dating or anything. I don't know." She huffs and rubs her palms over her pants. "Anyway." She smiles at me. "You going out of town for the holidays?"

"Holidays?" I muse, stuck on her fidgety actions.

She gives me a weird look. "Christmas, New Year's, you know, the holidays people typically spend with family."

"Oh." I force a chuckle. "I think I'll stick around."

"Really? No family get-togethers or anything? Won't your parents miss you?"

I shift on my feet. "Uh, no, probably not. They have a lot going on right now with my dad, and they won't be celebrating."

Her eyes bulge and her hand covers her mouth. "Oh my god. I'm so sorry. I forgot. He's sick or something, right?"

I nod my head, realizing I never mentioned what the family emergency was exactly. "Yeah."

"God, I'm really on a roll lately." Her cheeks redden. "You don't think you should...you know, spend time with him?"

Shit.

"Mom requested a relaxing environment for him, so..." I leave it there and switch the attention back to her. "What about you? Your family still lives here, right?"

She pushes her hair behind her shoulder. "Yeah. Well, kind of. They live forty minutes away, but they're gonna be in Mexico for Christmas. I'll be with them on New Year's Eve, so I'll be spending time with friends before then."

"That sounds nice."

"Yeah. My girlfriends and I will be staying in a Sugarbush cabin."

"Nice."

The door pushes open and in walks Kaspian. Snowflakes cling to his black hoodie and coat the bottom of his boots. He removes his hood and spots us both, his lips pulling up higher on one side.

"Hey, guys."

"Hey," Willow chirps, standing from her desk.

I lift my chin in greeting and he eye fucks me in return.

"How is everyone?" he asks in a teasing tone, surveying both of us as he slides his hands into his pockets.

"Fine," Willow answers quickly, scurrying around the desk without making eye-contact. "I'm going to go to the bathroom and then I'll be ready."

"Okay," he replies.

"And you?" he asks me while Willow's still making her way out of the room.

"Good. You?"

He takes a step closer, eyes flickering over my shoulder. "Can't complain." His face changes when she's gone, his eyes lowering and a salacious smile forming on his sinful lips. "It's too bad I can't have you for lunch."

"Can't you?" I counter, arching a brow.

"Can I?" His head tilts and his brows lift.

I force a tight grin. "You have plans. With Willow." I leave the statement there, knowing he hears the question in the words.

"Indeed, I do." I scrutinize him, waiting for more. He matches my silence for several seconds before he says, "Oh. Are you feeling a little envious?"

"Just as I said before, I'm curious. That's all. What's going on there?"

"Don't worry. I'm being smart."

He doesn't give me time to reply before he's right in front of me, his hand going to the back of my head while his tongue slides into my mouth.

It's easy to get lost in Kaspian, but I realize we can't get carried away here. Not now. So, I force myself to take a step back.

"Well, have fun," I tell him, right before Willow returns with her jacket on.

"Okay, I'm ready." She turns to face me as she stands next to Kaspian. "You sure you don't want to come?"

She gazes at me with a muted panic in her eyes. I can't

tell if she's trying to tell me she wants me to come or doesn't want me anywhere near them. Willow appears to be nervous.

"I'm fine," I say.

"You sure?" Kaspian asks this time. "We're going to this place that has a really good tossed salad."

I fight off my grin as Kaspian's lips quirk.

I shake my head. "I need a little more than that. Thanks, though."

He winks at me before turning and escorting Willow outside. She glances at me through the window as they walk off, something churning behind her eyes. I just don't know what.

CHAPTER THIRTY

" I heard she took off over problems with some guy, but somebody else said she had some personal family issues come up."

I gaze up at Shevon after she drops off my plate and listen to some more gossip about a girl who left town.

"Wow," I say, feigning interest.

"It's been a few weeks now, I think. I'm not sure. But nobody's heard a word from her. No social media posts or anything. Which is weird for young people these days, you know? Everybody wants everybody else to know what they're doing, even if it's bullshit—even if they're at a funeral."

"Yeah," I say with a nod, shoveling food into my mouth.

"Anyway, I'll be back to check on you soon."

Before I can get two full minutes of peace to eat my food, I hear, "Hey, lover," before Kaspian plops himself into the seat across from me.

I finish chewing my food and wipe my lips with a napkin. "What're you doing here?"

"You're here," he says simply, shrugging his shoulders.

225

"And where's Willow? How was your date yesterday?"

He laughs. "Date? I wouldn't say that."

"What do you talk about?"

"Different things. She asks about us quite a bit."

"What do you mean?"

"She seems to be curious about the workings of our relationship."

"Hmm."

Shevon appears next to the table with a glass of water she places in front of Kaspian. "Hey, will you be having dinner?"

"Sure," Kas replies. "I'll have the pad Thai Thanks."

"Of course. Anything else to drink?"

"No, I'm fine with water."

"I'll be back," she replies cheerfully.

"Has she asked you about us?" He picks right back up with our conversation.

"Yes, a couple times."

"Do you think she's suspicious that we're more than acquaintances?"

"Maybe," I answer before taking a sip of my drink. "But why would she care?"

He brings his hands to the tabletop, his tattooed fingers tapping on the wood. "You may not believe me, but I think she's into me."

I digest that information. Initially, I didn't think that was the case, but recently it seems more likely. "And what? She's jealous?"

He sits back, shrugging. "She knows I'm bi."

"She doesn't know about me."

"She might assume. You have to admit that when we're together we definitely have sexual energy charging between us. People might notice."

"So then maybe you should let her know it's not gonna happen between you two."

He lifts a brow, amusement in his expression. "Are we going steady?" he asks in a teasing tone.

Shevon shows up with Kaspian's plate of food and a refill of my Coke. "So, did you guys hear that Bill wasn't the only one cheating?" She dives right back into some gossip. "Kathy decided to do a little stepping out of her own. Probably in retaliation, not that I condone it, but..." she grins, giving us a shrug. "Sometimes people need a taste of their own medicine."

"Who?" Kaspian asks.

"I'll fill you in later."

"You guys need anything else?" Shevon asks.

"No. We're good," I answer.

"Who are Bill and Kathy?" Kas asks once she's gone.

"Some middle-aged couple that was here last time I was. Shevon likes to fill me in on the town gossip. Just like some guy left town after being caught with a teenage girl, and some other girl took off over a guy, or possibly family problems." I shake my head. "I don't care about any of it, but you gotta act like you do sometimes."

"There's too much going on in this small ass town."

I chew my food and take a drink before I speak again. "About Willow."

"Ah. Yes. You want me to stop going out with her because you're afraid she and I will fall in love and you'll be left out, right?"

I give him an unamused look. "I'm afraid you're going to get caught up in a situation that gets us both in trouble."

He puts his fork down and crosses his arms on the table. "You think I'm obsessed with her." He sounds frustrated. "Didn't you hear me when I said the women I was with prior to you were simply to get your attention? You think I can't control myself?"

"You killed them, didn't you?" I whisper harshly, leaning forward. "Were you in control then? How about when you nearly ripped that man's tongue from his mouth just for getting close to me? Is that being in control?"

He inhales deeply through his nose, his nostrils flaring as he exhales. "I was in control. I told you I didn't have a choice. She was onto me and was going to open her mouth and ruin everything I had been planning."

"And the other one from the library? The one you fucked and then..." I don't say the word out loud again. Too many ears. "Was that for me, too?"

"You saw me with her. Saw her disappear. So, yes," he answers smoothly. "A man has needs. I wasn't celibate because I wasn't sure what would happen between us. I didn't even know if you'd be into guys. I just knew I needed to know you. You can't be mad at that."

I blow out a frustrated breath. "You haven't told me what your plan with Willow is. I know you have one, and if it isn't to obsess over and fuck, then what is it? Because if anything happens to her, it won't be good for either of us."

He sighs. "I know. You've told me."

Shevon rushes over, her eyes wide. "Guys, I just heard about this girl who went missing."

"The one who had family problems?" I ask.

She shakes her head. "No, there was another one. Her name's Laura and she was fairly new here. Her aunt came to town to track her down because they had plans to meet up in New York for Thanksgiving. The aunt had been out of the country for work, and she couldn't get in touch with her niece when she returned. Thanksgiving came and went, so she finally tracked down the address where Laura was living. The apartment had been abandoned, but it was left like she had the intention of coming back. Nothing was packed, food was going bad in the fridge, and laundry was in the washer. She didn't appear to leave town to meet with her aunt. She's just gone. They've launched an investigation."

It takes everything in me to not stare at Kaspian with worry. "Oh wow. That's awful."

Shevon nods, looking solemn. "My friend who works at the library said she saw her there a few times, but never really spoke to her. Now she's gone. I wonder what happened."

My body tenses and I can tell Kaspian's stopped moving as well. "Hopefully they find her," I say, knowing they won't.

"I gotta get back to work, but apparently with this new information, they're going to start looking into the other girl's disappearance."

I nod my head slowly. "Good." Shevon walks off and I meet Kaspian's gaze. "Not good at all."

CHAPTER
THIRTY-ONE

K aspian leaves the restaurant shortly after the news, only saying, "I gotta go."

Days go by and he doesn't respond to any messages. I worry about his impulsive behavior because I'm not sure what he may do. Did he take off?

The local news has talked a little about the disappearance of these women. The cops are questioning friends and family and looking into the women's lives. Most people don't run away out of the blue. Unless, of course, you're a criminal.

Two pretty, young women going missing in the same small town raises eyebrows. People are on alert, and rumors are spreading like wildfire. Luckily, everything I've heard hasn't included Kaspian. He may need to show his face soon, though, or he'll make himself look suspicious.

I go by his job on my lunch break, hoping to find him there, but one of his co-workers tells me he took personal leave.

I shake my head, frustrated with his lack of communication, and head back to work. When I'm nearing my building, a cop car passes me, going in the opposite direction and I can't help but tense up. Hopefully he's not looking for Kaspian, too.

Inside, I take off my jacket and hang it up, finding Willow sitting on the small, teal-colored couch in the break room.

"You okay?"

She's zoned out, ignoring the sandwich on her lap. After a few seconds, her eyes find mine. "Oh. Yeah, I'm fine. Just thinking about all this stuff going on."

"What's that?" I ask, playing dumb.

"These women," she says with a bite in her tone, her eyebrows furrowing. "They're missing, Ezra."

I nod. "Right. It's awful."

She shakes her head like she's trying to calm down. "I'm sorry. It's just...they're my age, you know? Give or take a few years. I mean, how many more might go missing?"

I sit down next to her. "Maybe it's just a coincidence. I don't think you have anything to be worried about."

"You really think so?" she questions, her eyes searching mine.

"I'm hoping it's a coincidence, but no, I don't think anything will happen to you. Even if I have to make sure of it myself."

She gives me the smallest grin, but it falls fast. "Doesn't mean other women won't get killed."

My spine stiffens. "Killed?"

Willow's eyes snap to mine. "You can't possibly think they're still alive."

"We can hope."

She scoffs. "It's been weeks, Ezra."

"People have been found years later."

She gets up, tossing her food in the trash. "I don't

231

know." She whirls around and studies the floor before looking up at me. "I'm taking some leave. I'm gonna start my Christmas vacation early. I just want to spend a week in a cabin with my friends."

"That'll be nice," I say with a nod.

Something vibrates next to me. She left her phone on the couch, so I pick it up to hand it to her, but I freeze when I see the name on the screen.

Kaspian.

He doesn't seem to have a problem reaching out to her. What the hell?

She takes the phone and glances down at the message. Her face remains stoic, but then she looks up. "One of them was my friend. I hope she's alive. I really do. But I don't have a lot of hope." Her lips form a sad smile before she says, "I hope you have a good Christmas."

FUCKING CHRIST! A friend of Willow's. This just got a lot worse, and the fact that Kaspian is ignoring me is pissing me off. He just texted Willow, so I know he's not in hiding.

Without another plan, I decide I have to keep my eyes on Willow. Maybe they'll meet up and I'll be able to get to him. I need to know what he's up to and why he thinks it's a good idea to avoid me. Hopefully he's just making sure there's no connection to him. No evidence anywhere.

I never asked for details about what he did to these women. Or where. I assume it was at his house since he has the privacy and the land to dispose of them without getting the attention from anyone else. But if for some reason someone connects him to both of them, they could search his place.

After work, she goes straight home and doesn't leave. It's nearly eleven o'clock when I decide to go home with the plan of coming back in the morning. I'm on the street perpendicular to hers, parked behind an RV. Hopefully this is still here tomorrow because it offers cover while allowing me to see if anyone comes or goes.

I attempt to call Kaspian when I get home, but it goes to voicemail and I decide to quit trying. I go to sleep, wake up at five in the morning and head back to my hiding spot behind the RV near Willow's house.

It's mid-December and cold as fuck. Snow clings to my windows, thick flakes falling from the dark sky. We already have several inches on the ground, but I hear we're in for a winter storm. Based on how fast and how much snow is falling now, we're starting to feel the effects of it already.

The wind begins to pick up, eventually leading to a howling sound outside my window, whipping the flakes to the east and ruining their direct descent from the clouds.

I turn the heater up and use my windshield wipers to clear my front window. It's covered again in a matter of minutes. At nearly seven, people begin to stir. Windows open, outside lights turn off, and a few residents begin to scrape the snow from their cars to get ready for work.

A snowplow drives past me and I'm grateful that I have the day off. I listen to the weather report and hear them talk about how the worst is yet to come. In the next few hours, we'll have nearly a foot dumped on us. Non-essential businesses are choosing to stay closed and the anchors are telling people to stay home unless travel is necessary.

Just as they say that, I notice movement at Willow's place. I clear my window and spot her in a large jacket, holding a suitcase as she runs to her car. She's trying to get to her cabin before the roads are too bad.

Once she's got the snow off her windows, she jumps in and pulls out onto the street. I debate on whether it's necessary to follow her. She's going to a cabin with her friends for the week. After that, she's spending time with her family. Going up there won't lead me to Kaspian.

I begin to back up and pull out from behind the RV when I notice another car turn the corner and drive behind her.

It's Kaspian. He's in the second truck he had parked at his property. She won't know it's him even if she was paying attention. The snow will make it hard to make anybody out anyway.

I have no choice now. I follow him as he follows her.

CHAPTER
THIRTY-TWO

The drive isn't too bad. My truck is built for the winter conditions, but I have to make sure Kaspian doesn't notice me, so I let them get ahead.

I remember where she said she was going, so even if I can't follow directly behind, I know where to go. All I have to do is look for their vehicles once I'm there.

I can't help but wonder what Kaspian's plan is. Why is he following her? Does he know that one of the girls was her friend? Is he planning on killing her too? But why?

I drum my fingers on the steering wheel; something in the road has us at a standstill for a while. When we get moving again, I come across a sign for Sugarbush Resort. However, I haven't seen any cars turn off. Did she miss the exit?

I decide to keep going straight and eventually spot Kaspian's truck. We go all the way to Stowe, which is about forty-five minutes from Sugarbush. She lied about where she was going.

Keeping my distance, I do my best to get an idea of

where she might be heading without having to follow directly.

She turns to the right, as does Kaspian. If he's trying to be secretive about tailing her, this isn't the best way to do it. There aren't many cars traveling in the same direction now that we're off the highway and getting closer to rental cabins.

I keep going straight with the plan to circle back once they're out of sight. Nearly ten minutes later, I find my way back to where they turned off and travel through some rough roads. The snow is piling up, and there doesn't appear to have been any plowing done yet. These roads are less traveled, so they'll be done much later than the main ones. I pass a few cabins. There's about forty or fifty yards between them, giving the sense of privacy while also being able to see the one next to you.

However, I realize it's a dead-end road, and the last cabin is backed up to several massive trees with open space in the front. It's much larger than I expected, but probably the perfect size for a girls' trip. The cabin is made up of windows, giving the occupants next to no privacy. Good thing there's only one neighbor since they scored the last cabin on the road; at least they won't have people watching from every angle.

I stop at the cabin before Willow's so she doesn't spot my truck. Luckily, it doesn't appear to be occupied, so I pull up on the opposite side, hiding most of my vehicle from the view of her cabin.

Her car is already parked as close to the front door as she can get, but what's surprising is that so is Kaspian's.

They're the only two there. No friends. Just them.

I step around the corner, straining to get a good look at the cabin through the falling snow, but thanks to all the windows on every side of their place, I get a good shot of them embracing in the middle of the living room.

He didn't follow her here. She invited him.

I WENT BACK to the nearest town to grab some small grocery items plus a few other necessities before driving back to the cabin. Luckily, nobody arrived while I was out, so I finagle my way in through a weak lock on a door that leads to the laundry room.

After a quick peek around, I determine nobody's staying here. There's no luggage in any of the rooms or food in the fridge. Hopefully the storm will keep people away for the time being.

I only brought a few bottles of water and some food that doesn't require much cooking. I have a couple frozen dinners that only need a microwave and a plastic fork. I don't plan on being here long. I just need to know what the hell is going on across the way. I pull out the pair of binoculars I bought at the store and make my way to the window above the kitchen sink. I spot Willow in front of the stove, cooking them a meal. Kaspian's nowhere in sight.

Hours go by without anything happening. They're acting like a couple on vacation, except I haven't seen them doing anything sexual yet. If it were me and Kaspian, we'd have fucked in three different places already. All they're doing is laughing, talking, eating, and watching TV. When they pull out the wine, I sit on the kitchen counter while I wait for my dinner to cook.

Am I wasting my time by being here? Something in me says I need to be close. If Kaspian finds out one of the girls he killed was friends with Willow, he might panic and kill her. If he does that, we're both in trouble.

However, the idea that they fled out here to have alone time together rubs me the wrong way. I know for a fact if the roles were reversed, Kaspian would be camped outside the cabin, too. He'd be furious and ready to pounce. Why does he get to get away with it?

The microwave dings and I pull out the black plastic tray with chicken and mashed potatoes and eat up. It's not great, but it's something. Once I'm done, I toss it into one of my plastic grocery bags to take with me later.

Another peek through the binoculars sets me on edge.

They're on the couch. Willow has her hand on his thigh, laughing about something. They're too close. Too close for friendship. Too close for my liking.

She takes his wine glass and travels back to the kitchen where she pours him another glass. He rubs his hands over his knees, staring straight ahead. Something about his posture looks tense. I angle the binoculars in her direction and find her strutting back to Kaspian with two glasses in hand. They clink them together and drink.

Willow puts hers down on the coffee table before moving quickly and pressing her mouth to his. In a flash, Kaspian has her pinned beneath him.

I put the binoculars down, grab what I need, and throw my jacket back on before I make my way through the heavy snow to get to their cabin.

THIRTY-THREE

The snow is well past my ankles, creeping up my shins as I begin my trek to the trees that rest ten yards behind the back of the cabin. The combination of night and snow gives me enough cover within the thicket to feel comfortable that nobody will see me. All of their lights are on inside, giving me a perfect view while obstructing theirs.

When I get to the trees behind their log chalet, I attempt to find their figures, but can't see them anywhere. Perhaps they went upstairs. I don't dwell on what they very well could be in the middle of doing. My rage keeps me warm as the blizzard swarms around me.

Wind whips snow against my face, the flakes clinging to my lashes. I storm forward, making my way to the back door. It's locked, but if it's similar to the lock at my cabin, I know I can get in.

I peer through the glass square in the door, but there's no movement. No noise either. With a mini screwdriver I purchased earlier today, I use it for the second time and get the door to unlock. I pause, waiting for someone to say something, but I'm met with silence.

I turn the knob, careful to not make any noise, and push the door open slowly. After taking a step inside, I close the door quietly and travel deeper into the house, turning off a couple lights as I go. No need to chance anyone else seeing inside.

The fire in the living room burns bright enough to give off a warm glow, and I make my way toward the stairs. I follow the sound of hushed voices, hoping my steps don't make the stairs squeak.

On the second floor, I come to stop and listen intently.

"What do you think about..." The rest is muffled, whispered.

"I'm not sure." Kaspian's voice.

"Did you ever..."

I creep closer to the closed door they're behind.

"Who?" Kaspian asks.

"Emerson."

Silence. "I don't know who that is."

"Oh. You sure?"

Shuffling. "I don't know who you're talking about," he replies calmly.

I'm met with more silence. I press my ear to the door and hear what sounds like kissing. I put my hand on the knob, ready to turn it and push it open. I want to know what the hell is going on. I'm ready to kill them both at this point.

Kaspian has the nerve to run off with my co-worker for a week of sex, all while ignoring me, knowing he'd absolutely lose his shit if the tables were turned. His need to be wanted and desired is too strong. He needs attention from more than just me.

Willow, on the other hand, is hard to crack. She made it clear she was attracted to Kaspian, but then she said they were just friends. She shows up to my house talking nonsense before kissing me. She tells me she's going to one cabin, just to go to another one. Not with friends as she said, but with Kaspian. Kaspian, who belongs to me.

"Does he know?" she asks quietly.

"Does who know what?"

The silence stretches on, seemingly lasting forever before she finally says, "Ezra."

My hackles raise at the mention of my name, my body tensing, ears straining.

"What does he need to know?" Kaspian asks.

Silence. Silence. Silence.

"That you killed Emmy."

My eyes widen as my heart throws itself at my ribcage. Behind the door, the bed creaks with movement and I hear Kaspian say, "Wait!"

I throw open the door, ripping a scream from Willow's throat. I find her on top of Kaspian wearing only a shirt and panties while Kas lies underneath her in his typical white tank top that he wears under his T-shirts. In her hand is a knife, ready to plunge into his heart. Her eyes are red-rimmed and wild.

"What're you doing here?" she asks, her weapon suspended in the air above his chest.

"What are *you* doing?" I fire back.

"You don't understand, Ezra. He killed my friend. I know he did. He's not who you think he is. I've been watching him. He was the last person to see Emerson. She spent time with him at her job. He was there constantly. I saw the security camera footage. And then she went miss-

241

ing. The other girl too. The one who's sister came looking for her. It was him. It has to be."

She's a mess of emotions—anger, sadness, and frustration swirling together, making her voice high and demeanor agitated.

I step forward, holding my hands up. "It's okay. You don't want to do this."

"Yes, I do," she cries. "Emmy was one of my best friends. She was a sweet girl, and I knew she liked him. She mentioned some guy she was talking to, but never said his name. It's him. He did this. Why?" she screams, looking into Kaspian's eyes.

I take another step closer. "Tell the cops," I say. Kaspian's eyes flicker to mine. "If it's true, tell the cops."

"I almost did," she says. "They questioned me, but I don't have proof. They wouldn't be able to do anything."

"They could look into the tapes. They could search his house. You don't want to become a killer."

She presses the tip of the kitchen knife to his sternum. She doesn't realize the breastbone is hard to penetrate. "Maybe I do. He doesn't deserve to live." Her breaths come in heavy pants, her shoulders rising and falling as she struggles with her morality.

"You'll go to jail."

Her eyes fly to mine. "You weren't supposed to be here."

"And yet, here I am. What're you gonna do, Willow? Kill us both?"

"I never wanted you to be involved," she cries. "But you knew him, and I needed a way to get close. I wanted him to want me. I hoped he'd try to make me his next victim."

That explains a few things.

"Instead, he's about to be yours. Maybe you're wrong about him."

She shakes her head, her hair falling around her face. "I'm not." She stares down at Kaspian. "Admit it, you piece of shit. Admit you killed her!"

Kas shakes his head slightly, his body still beneath her. "I didn't."

Willow's petite. Easy enough to push off, but he remains motionless, like he's afraid of her. I know it's not true; he's trying to play the part of the victim. He'll plead his innocence until she stabs him.

She screams, her frustration at its peak. "Yes, you fucking did! You know how I know? Because I found her bracelet in your car. The jewelry of mine that you admired so much? Yeah, she was one of the friends who helped me make them. I know that bracelet. We made it together and it was lodged between your seats! She was with you. You killed her, then you went about your life like nothing happened. You're a freak. A fucking sicko. You—"

I'm behind her in a second, my arm around her chest while my other hand reaches for her wrist. I can't listen to her talk about him like this. I refuse. "Now, Willow."

"No!" she screeches as I begin to pull her off of him.

Her hand moves in a downward arc, the blade slashing across his ribs before I can wrap her in my arms completely.

My eyes watch the blood spill from the gash, turning the white cotton of his shirt a dark crimson. I connect with his gaze. Shock blankets his face as he looks down at the blood. Willow struggles in my grasp but I squeeze tighter.

"What did you do?" I whisper.

"He deserves it! He deserves worse! He's a fucking monster, Ezra. He's fucked up."

I spin her around and knock the knife from her hand. It clatters to the floor just as I shove her against one of the

243

four wood posts surrounding the bed. My hand squeezes her jaw as she looks at me with frightened eyes.

"So am I," I seethe. "I'm all those things you just said. Maybe even more so. I do it because I like the way it makes me feel. He killed her for me, and I won't let you take him away."

"No, no," she says, shaking her head as tears pool in her eyes.

"Yes. You should've left him alone, Willow. Now you've fucked up. I was trying to save you. I didn't want you to be hurt, but now you've hurt him, and he's the only thing in this world that's ever brought me any semblance of happiness."

Her body vibrates with fear, tears streaking down her face. "I don't—"

I pull the knife from my back pocket, ready to drive it into her body over and over. She cut him. She tried to kill him. She can't live any longer.

Right before I'm about to plunge it into her stomach, I feel Kaspian's hand on mine. "No."

I angle my head and find him standing behind me, his left hand pressing against the wound as his right hand holds my wrist.

"What?"

"Don't be so impulsive." He tries to smirk, but the pain is too much. "Get her on the bed."

I bring her around, and he yanks the comforter to the floor. Considering it's got his blood on it, that makes sense.

Willow whimpers and struggles while I get her on top of the sheets, straddling her the way she straddled him.

"She couldn't take it anymore," Kaspian whispers. "The disappearance and possible death of her best friend. She came up here to end it all."

Willow screams and I clamp my hand over her mouth, not that anyone will be able to hear her, but so I'm able to think. She wriggles underneath me, kicking her legs and twisting her body, but I'm too heavy to move.

"Grab the knife she had. There's a scarf on the dresser. Wipe your blood from it and bring it here."

Kas moves slowly, but he does it. When I go to reach for it, he shakes his head. "She tried killing me."

With a swift motion, the blade slides from the middle of her forearm to her wrist, parting the skin. She screams into my palm, her body bucking. I hold her arm down, allowing the blood to pour out. Kaspian moves to the other side and struggles to keep her arm down so he can do the same thing. Every movement he makes hurts based on the expressions on his face, but he eventually slices the blade down the same path, moving his hand to grip her upper arm so she doesn't spray blood all over both of us.

It's not quick. It takes a while to bleed out. But after a while, her body loses some strength and she's no longer fighting. Her skin turns pale, but she's still breathing. Barely.

I glance over at Kaspian and find him on the floor, slumped against the wall, his face set in a grimace. I jump off of Willow and make my way to him. She doesn't move. She's no longer a threat, but now my focus is on Kas.

"Let me see."

"I'm fine," he grunts.

"Looks like it."

I move his hand and lift the undershirt, trying to get a look at the cut. I find his black tee on the floor and bring it over to wipe the blood away. He hisses in pain, but I have to see what we're working with here.

It's about four inches long and deep enough to require

stitches. No major arteries were severed which is good, but he's still losing a good amount of blood.

"You're gonna be okay."

"You sure?"

I grab his face and make him look into my eyes. "You're not allowed to leave me. You understand?" I shove the T-shirt against the wound and find the scarf from earlier and tie it tightly around his torso.

"Sounds like you care."

"I'm here, aren't I? Why would that be?"

His eyes study my face. "I was going to kill her. That's why I'm here. Not for any other reason."

"Good, because I was already thinking about killing you for being here with her."

He snorts. "I knew she was on to me. I took some time to look into the girls and found out she knew one of them. We were both playing a part. I didn't expect her to have a knife hidden under the pillow. She got to it before I could play out my plan." He sucks in a breath. "The situation escalated faster than I wanted it to."

"It's okay," I say. "I have to find some things. Stay here. Keep pressing down."

I get up and run to the bathroom but don't find what I'm looking for. In the bathroom downstairs I find a first-aid kit, and in another bedroom I find a sewing kit in a drawer.

I run back to Kaspian. "This is gonna hurt, but we have to stop the bleeding."

His eyes find what's in my hands. "Great."

After removing the shirt and scarf, I use the peroxide and antiseptic wipes to clean the area. The small teal-blue box has a few needles, a couple spools of thread, and some buttons, but it's enough. I thread the needle and look into his eyes.

"Ready?"

He looks away and I take that as a yes. I pinch together his skin and stick the needle through his flesh, threading it to the other side. I repeat this for the length of the wound, all while Kaspian cusses and grunts, banging his fist against the wall.

"Jesus fuck!"

"I gotta do it again."

He sighs, but I keep it moving. I have to do another passthrough to make sure it stays closed, trying to move as fast as I can. Once I'm done, I put some gauze over the wound and use some large Band-Aids to keep them in place.

"Okay," I say. "I have to clean up. We're gonna have to take the comforter with us. I'll wash the glass you used, and then I'll wrap her hand around the knife before I drop it to the floor. Luckily we have time. Nobody will be making their way up here anytime soon, but we have to move your truck and find somewhere else to stay."

"Quintin," he says softly.

"You're gonna be in pain, but we have to move. Do you think you can drive? I'll follow you into town. We should go before even more snow falls."

"Quin."

"What?"

He reaches for my hand. "Thank you."

I give it a squeeze. "Don't fucking do that to me again. I can't exist in a world where you don't."

His lips pull up in the corners. "You're so obsessed with me."

I lean down and press a kiss to his mouth. "You wouldn't want it any other way."

KASPIAN

THIRTY-FOUR

The rest of the night flies by. I lie helpless on the floor while Quin runs around cleaning up any of my blood that dripped to the floor. Thankfully they aren't carpet, assuring the cleanup is an easy task. He uses two thirty-gallon trash bags to secure the comforter before grabbing another one from the linen closet and laying it across the bottom of the bed. He washes the wine glass I drank from before putting it back in the cabinet.

His gloves remained on the entire time, but he still made it a point to wipe down anything I told him I touched. Everything was put back in its place and made to look like Willow came up here alone to drink and take her own life.

Quin took her phone and typed up a message in her notes to really sell the idea. We have at least a week before we have to worry about her being found. The storm is supposed to last another couple days, and it'll probably be a few days before plows make their way out here. After that, it'll depend on what her friends decide to do. How long until they alert the police? The silver lining in her trying to lure me up here to kill me is that she likely didn't tell anyone where she was going.

"Okay, gotta get you to your truck and hope the snow eventually hides the fact that you were parked here to begin with. It's gonna hurt, but you'll need to follow me until we get to a hotel. Maybe twenty minutes."

I nod. "Okay. Help me up."

With a parting glance at a very pale Willow on the bed, we make our way out of the bedroom and down the stairs where he remembers to re-lock the back door.

"You followed me," I say as he grabs my shoes and jacket and helps me get them on.

"Of course. You were ignoring me and I found out Willow was friends with one of the girls. I figured you'd find out and do something stupid."

"She did a good job at pretending she liked me, but it would slip. I'd catch her looking at me like she hated me. When I knew she saw those tapes at Perfectly Convenient, I knew I had to kill her. She would've messed up everything for us. I know you're worried about the police coming around, but—"

"I know. Don't worry. We'll figure something out."

"The security tapes shouldn't be a problem soon. They normally keep them from thirty to ninety days. Since Willow saw them, it's definitely more than thirty, but we should be approaching the retention requirements."

He pulls the hood over my head. "I said we'll figure it out."

Quin gets me and our evidence into my truck, and I thank whatever deity there may be that I got a truck fit for this weather, but it's still a pain to get through the snow. I stop at the cabin he broke into so he can clean up after himself there. It doesn't take long before he's getting into his own truck with another trash bag.

We make our way into the nearest town, thankful that the main roads have been plowed a little. Quin pulls into a hotel and disappears inside before running back out to my window.

"No vacancy. Next one is a few miles down. Don't use your phone. Just follow me."

When we approach the next hotel, he keeps driving. This place is ripe with resorts and inns, but he's clearly looking for a specific type. My side burns and throbs, but I breathe through the pain until he pulls into a small place.

When he returns to my car, he sighs. "Okay, we're gonna be here. It's the only place that gives us our own little townhouse and we don't have to see other guests or be in huge resorts with a million cameras. It's around the corner. Follow me."

A couple minutes later, we pull into a small parking space in front of something that looks like a cottage. There's several of the same cookie cutter buildings around us, but at least this one is just for me and him.

We settle into the room, finding we have a kitchenette, flat screen TV, and queen-sized bed to go along with a blue loveseat and two end tables. The cream-colored walls are covered in hand painted photos of what looks like the house we're staying in, plus buildings from the town about a hundred years ago. The burgundy carpet runs through the townhouse, matching the thick valance and panel sets on the windows.

"Looks like a place for a grandma, but it's nice enough."

Quin removes his jacket and shoes, inspecting them closely. "I'll have to get rid of these. There's blood on them."

"At least they're black and nobody could tell."

He rips off his shirt and unbuttons his pants. "I have to shower. Need help with anything?"

"Can you help get this jacket off me?" I ask, dragging my heels on the carpet to loosen my boots and toe them off.

Quin comes around and removes my jacket with caution. To keep me from having to extend my arms to get my undershirt off, Quin uses the tear in the bloodied material and rips it completely in half. He does the best he can to keep me from moving too much, but I wince and hiss as the remaining scraps of my shirt are taken off me.

Standing up, I pull the covers back on the bed before turning to face him. "I may pass out before you get out."

"Then let me help you out of these," he says, reaching out to unbutton my jeans.

He drops down into a crouch as he pulls the material down, allowing me to step out of them. His eyes meet mine.

"You look good down there. Maybe I sleep naked."

He smirks. "You're too hurt to play these games."

"Not even a blow job? I think I've earned one."

"No." He stands up and tosses my jeans on the couch. "Get some rest. I'll check on that later. I don't have any pain killers but maybe I can find some tomorrow."

"You know what might help?" I ask, sitting on the mattress before I attempt to lay down and scoot over. My flirtatious remark dies on my tongue as pain settles in. "Oh fuck. Never mind. Just forget it." I grimace as I try to settle into a decent position.

He chuckles before heading to the bathroom. I don't know how much time goes by, but at some point, I feel the covers pull back and cold air hits my torso. Quin's fingers graze the area around my bandage before he feels my forehead.

"Still alive," I murmur.

He covers me back up and makes his way to his side of the bed. "Good."

CHAPTER
THIRTY-FIVE

We've been here for two days, and through the entire forty-eight hours, Quin is in and out, getting us food, picking up some pain killers for me as well as new bandages, and keeping me up-to-date on the road conditions. My wound is still ugly but doesn't seem to be showing signs of infection. Probably thanks to Quin's constant checks.

The news hasn't mentioned anything about Willow's death, so she still hasn't been discovered, nor reported missing. We know we're on borrowed time, but he hasn't mentioned anything about what we're going to do going forward.

"Hey," I say as we lounge on the bed watching the news. "What's the plan?"

He scoots up and leans against the headboard, taking a deep breath. "I already called my job and told them I had to quit. I had a story I told Jason about my dad being sick, so I'm running with that. There will be proof that it was brought up previously, so if anyone ever questions it, he'll be able to say, 'Yeah, he mentioned it in October.' They weren't exactly thrilled because with all this snow they need all the workers they can get, but how can you argue with someone who's dad is in the hospital?

"So, the story for me is my dad is sick, probably dying, and I have to move back home to help my mom. I called my landlord with the same story and said I would be by to grab all personal effects and will arrange a moving company to pick up furniture whenever he can be there to supervise. I offered to pay rent for the next two months, so he can have enough time to get a new tenant."

"Okay. I should've known you've been planning everything out. Where are you moving? And where does that leave me?"

"I'm not sure where yet, but you're coming with me. Obviously."

I grin. "Obviously, huh?"

"I'm not going to leave you to the wolves. If the cops are good at their jobs they may connect you to the women who've gone missing, but just because you were at the store where one worked and at a library with the other doesn't mean you're the only person to be there with them. There's no real proof. Where are the bodies?"

"Gone. Far far away and not near my house."

He nods. "You'll have to sell your place and quit your job."

"Won't it look suspicious that we're both moving at the same time? Suddenly, and right after women start disappearing?"

"I don't give a fuck what it looks like. I care whether we get caught or not. We can tell people we're together. It would make sense for you to come with me while I deal with the impending death of my father."

I can't help but smile wider. "We're going to tell people we're together? Like who?"

He gives me a look. "You shouldn't be focused on that part of the plan." His lips twitch slightly, though, telling me he's amused. "I'll tell Jason. He'll tell everyone. I don't talk to many other people."

"Well, I don't need much from my place. Just clothing and a few other small things. I'll contact an agent to do the sale without me having to stick around. Give them the same type of story."

"So, tonight we can leave and head back into town to grab everything we need and load it up. We'll need to drive to another nearby town and get you sewn up by a professional. We can say you got cut in the middle of the storm but we couldn't get to a hospital until now, which will explain the botched job."

"It's not that bad."

"You should still get it looked at." He takes a breath and then says, "What do you think about new identities?"

"Think we should?" I ask. He gives me a one-shoulder shrug. "I'm sorry. I know you were settled into Ezra Hamilton —the normal, regular citizen of a small town who isn't a killer."

He angles his head to stare at me. "I was never that. You should know. And I don't care who I have to become, because I'll always be Quintin Black to me—and to you. That'll never change. I can slip on a mask and a new personality wherever we go as long as I know I can be myself with you when I get back home."

"You're starting to sound a little domesticated," I tease. "Sounds a lot like a certain four-letter word to me."

"Fake?"

I throw my head back with a laugh. "Yeah."

His lips pull up on one side as he looks back at the TV. "We can figure out where to go and who we'll be later."

"And in the meantime..." I say, inching my way closer to him and trying not to wince. The pain has been easier to bear, and though it still hurts, I can't stay away from him much longer. "I was thinking since I showered and I'm feeling better, maybe we could..."

He arches a brow at me. "We could what?"

"You know," I say, reaching under his shirt.

"You think I can't see you hiding the fact that you're in pain?"

"Since when did my being in pain stop you from fucking me?"

"Since it wasn't me who inflicted it. Since it was a cut meant to take you from me. And I'm still not convinced those fake stitches won't come apart and have you bleeding all over the bed."

I bite into my lip before saying, "But you like blood."

"I don't like evidence."

Slowly, I attempt to get onto my knees, but I'm unable to keep from making a face. I power through. "Are you saying you don't want me?" I ask, reaching for the button of his jeans. "Are you saying you can't fuck me because of a little cut on my side?" I pull the zipper down. "Don't treat me like a doll now. Not unless it's a sex doll. I'm a big boy, Quintin. I can handle you."

His nostrils flare as he breathes. "Kaspian." He's warning me, his tone low and deep.

"Hmm?"

"You can't handle the way I want to fuck you right now."

"No?"

He grabs my wrist, his grip tight. "No. Because I want to

258

fuck you for many reasons. I want to fuck you to punish you. You shouldn't have gone off on your own without telling me what you were up to. You shouldn't have ignored me. I'm still so pissed that I could've..." He stops talking, his chest heaving with deep breaths. *Lost you*. That's what he was going to say. I know it. "You don't get to set rules for me and not adhere to any of your own." He pokes me in my chest. Right where his name is. "You belong to me. Remember that. I always get to be in the know. It's not like I'm going to judge you. I'm going to try to help."

I nod once, my chin dipping slowly. "Okay."

He shakes his head. "I want to fuck you so hard and so deep in the hope that you'll understand how much I do want you. So you'll know never to pull any stupid shit again. I need you to know without a doubt that you only need me. I want to mark and ruin you. I want to hurt you while making you feel so fucking good. I want to rip you apart just to be the one to put you together again, because I want you to know that I'm capable of both. Don't ask me to fuck you right now. I won't be able to control myself."

He watches me, waiting for my response. I can see the desire in his eyes. He wants the pleasure he receives from inflicting pain. He isn't capable of articulating his feelings. He likes to act like he doesn't have them, and maybe that's true, but he has them when it comes to me. I hear the unspoken words on the tip of his tongue when he kisses me. I feel his emotions when he lets loose and fucks me like an animal. He talks to me through his body and I'm an eager listener.

"Do what you want to me," I say. "Punish me. Teach me a lesson. Teach me many. I want you to lose control because it's when I like you most."

THIRTY-SIX

"Oh fuck," I cry as he flips me over.

On my hands and knees, he drives into me from behind, holding my hips with a tight grip. He's in control of my body, slamming my ass into him as he forces me to be impaled by his cock. I squeeze the pillow in my hands, falling to my elbows as he brutalizes me in the best fucking way.

One hand wraps around my throat, pulling me back up, his hips moving back and forth while his fingers dig into my neck.

He's nothing but grunts and growls—no longer a man. He's succumbed to every basic need. His noises are carnal, and he's turned me into a heap of moans and whimpers.

"Oh god," I moan, straightening my back until I touch his chest. He hooks his arm over the crook of my elbow, his hand traveling between us until he latches his fingers on my other arm, trapping me in place. He squeezes my throat, his lips touching my ear.

"You like the way I fuck you, don't you?"

"You know I do."

"Tell me you need me."

"I fucking need you."

"Who do you belong to?"

"You. Fuck," I breathe. "You, Quintin. I'm yours."

He thrusts deep. "Damn right you are. In this life and the next."

"Ah!" I cry. "Your cock feels so good."

He shoves me forward and I catch myself with my hands, barely noticing the pain in my side. Quin spreads my cheeks apart, watching himself push in and out of me with slower thrusts.

A low growl rumbles in his throat. "Mm. The way you stretch around me is like a dream."

I drop my head and let his words roll over me. He runs his hand up my back before his fingers thread into my hair, yanking my head up.

"I wanna come deep in your ass. I want every drop of me to be inside you."

"Oh yeah," I moan in agreement.

"But first, I want my cock in your mouth."

"Mmm. Okay."

Quin pulls out, his fingers pressing into my asshole. I drop my torso to the mattress, arching my ass as high into the air as I can get it while he continues to play with me. I mewl like a baby animal, enjoying every second of his touch.

He gets caught up in the moment, putting a pause on getting his dick sucked, then I feel his tongue in my ass.

"Oh shit!" I cry.

His hands spread me apart and he tongues the hell out of my hole, licking and prodding. His tongue slips inside for a second before he pulls back and his finger replaces it. He takes his time switching between the magic of his mouth and hand, driving me crazy with need. My cock throbs and leaks, desperate for a release.

"Quin," I breathe. "Baby. Oh fuck. It's so good. So fucking good."

He moans. "Don't come."

"I need to," I whine.

"No." He pulls away from me, pushing against my hip to flip me over to my back. "Spin around."

I rotate my body until my head is at the foot of the bed, his cock poised above my face. He cups a hand behind my neck and pulls me lower, until my head isn't fully on the mattress, and then he takes his shaft in hand and presses his crown to my lips.

"Open wide."

I drop my jaw, and then he's sliding across my tongue and touching the back of my throat. He fucks my mouth as I reach back and hold onto his thighs, grunting between his pleasure-filled noises. I gag and drool around him, giving him the sloppiest blow job, but one he seems to enjoy.

He pulls out, holding his shaft, and my saliva drips from his cock and back into my mouth. He teases me, pushing the tip between my lips before pulling out, and repeating the motion for several seconds.

"You want to swallow my dick?" he asks, smearing my spit across my lips with his head.

"Yes," I moan desperately.

"Mm."

He braces himself on the bed, rocking his hips and penetrating my mouth. His warm hand wraps around my cock and I nearly cry in relief. My dick weeps with need. I thrust into his grip as I choke on his cock.

"Such a needy boy."

I whimper, slurping around his erection.

Quin leans across my body and then I'm enveloped in his wet mouth. I gasp, or at least attempt to while my lips are stretched around him.

He swirls his tongue around my head, tasting the arousal that's been steadily leaking out of me. His lips close around my shaft and travel downwards, his hand on my balls, giving them a gentle massage.

"Fuck," I mumble around him. "Yes."

It's the first time he's had my dick in his mouth, and it's so fucking good I don't know how we'll survive, because this is all I'll ever want to do.

He strokes and sucks in tandem, working me over with a swiftness that would be embarrassing if he hadn't been fucking me for nearly half an hour already. My cock is ready to explode, and it's not going to take much more.

I bring my hand up and grab his dick, pulling it from my mouth. "Quin. You're gonna make me come."

All he does is up the speed of his hand and the flicker of his tongue around my head. His mouth comes off me just long enough to say, "Give it to me. Every. Last. Drop. Fill my mouth with your desire and coat my throat. I want the taste of you to last all day."

"Oh fuck."

Cum shoots from my tip like it was simply waiting for his permission. As soon as the words left his lips, my release shot between them.

I squeeze his thighs, my body tense and flexing as he makes sure to drink everything I give him. Once I'm completely spent, he backs up and lifts my head, bending down to slide his tongue into my mouth.

"Don't you taste good?"

I greedily suck on his tongue as I hold onto his face, moaning like a wanton slut. And maybe I am. For him.

When he pulls away, I spin around and lie on my back, watching him crawl between my legs with his heavy cock in his hand. He pushes my left thigh back as I hold the other one. Bringing his hand to his mouth, he spits on his fingers and presses them into me before pushing his wet cock into my hole.

Quintin leans over me, chest to chest, his thrusts bringing him in slow and deep. His eyes stare into mine, sending me messages he's unable to speak. In them, I see what I've always wanted—his need for me. His yearning. His obsession. But I also see the darkness and devilry, and I welcome it all.

I trace the scars on my chest that spell out his name and look him in the eye. "Yours."

His eyes close and his back bows as he finds his bliss. His cock twitches inside me, and he bellows into the room, cussing and calling to a god.

While he tries catching his breath, he leans his forehead on mine, mixing his sweat with my own.

"I don't believe in much," he says. "But I believe you were made for me."

I grin and my heart sings. "It's me and you," I tell him. "Until the end."

THIRTY-SEVEN

We didn't get to leave as soon as we had planned, but not everything goes according to plan, does it? Once we left our little cottage, we traveled to another nearby town to get stitched up, and it's already looking a lot better. Plus, I can move with ease now.

Our homes have already been packed up with everything we're willing to bring with us, and the loose ends of our jobs are tightened up. Quin thought it would be best to stop by his job to talk to his boss and appear *normal*. He wanted to thank him for understanding, and take some time to explain his made-up family problems so it would seem more genuine if anyone ever asks.

I could've and would've left my job without a word, but he insisted that would come across strange, so I listened. I told them my boyfriend had to leave town because of a death in the family, and the hopeless romantic that I am couldn't let him be alone in this dark time. They looked at me funny, unaware of a boyfriend, but it's not like I tell people my business.

Boyfriend. It's a label we'll need for some situations, but it doesn't feel right to me. He's hardly a boy and much more than a friend. There isn't a word for what we are to each other. He's everything to me. How do you encompass so much into a single word? I'd cease to live without him. I wouldn't want to walk this earth if it wasn't with him by my side. He's become much more than a desire. I want him, sure, but more than that, I *need* him. I need the acceptance he gives me. The cool detachment he often has feeds my obsessive side, forcing me to find a way to get him to show me something, even if it's necessary to make him jealous. He'll fuck me and claim me and whisper threats in my ear if I ever do it again. It breathes life into both of us. He needs to expel that energy just as I need to ingest it.

We're not normal by any means, and never claim to be. We need the toxicity. We need to feel the sting of pain from each other while also inflicting it. There's not another person in the world for either of us. How ironic to find solace in a man who initially brought you distress. He took from me what I had wanted for years—the death of my father. I hungered for revenge before eventually realizing I was just hungry for him.

Now, we're showing our faces at Thai Me Down one last time so Shevon can see us, hear our story, and eventually spread it to everyone in town.

"Hey, guys," she greets, putting her hands on her hips as she peers down at us with a wide smile. "How you been? You haven't been in this week, which is weird for you," she says with a chuckle aimed at Quin.

"We've been good," I answer with a grin.

"We've been spending a lot of time at my place lately," Quin adds, gazing at me with a love-struck expression to sell our relationship.

"Oh. Umm." She shifts on her feet, her finger gesturing between us. "Are you two a thing?"

I laugh. "Yeah."

She crosses her arms in front of her chest, staring at Quin. "Well, dang, you could've told me. It would've helped my ego and explained why you never asked me out." She winks at him, letting us know she's teasing.

People see men in a relationship and assume gay, never bi. In this case, their assumptions will help us. Why would we ever want a woman when we had each other?

Quin chuckles, but quickly changes his face so he looks a little forlorn. "Unfortunately, my dad has taken a turn for the worse. My mom really needs my help, since it doesn't look like he has much time. We're not gonna be in town much longer."

Shevon's face falls. "Oh no. I'm so sorry. I'll pray for him and your family. Will you ever come back?"

He shrugs. "Not sure." After a sigh and a swipe at his brow, he says, "So, we're gonna try to get there before the holidays and maybe get one more Christmas in."

She touches his shoulder, giving it a squeeze. "At least you have someone by your side," she says, glancing over at me with a small smile.

"I'll take care of him."

When she disappears to get our food, Quin exhales. "Well, the whole town should know in two to three days."

I laugh. "Definitely. Good acting."

He rolls his eyes.

Once we're done eating, we leave the restaurant and run directly into Jason.

"Hey! I was gonna text you."

"What's going on?" Quin asks, shoving his hands in the pockets of his jacket.

"Not much. We're gonna be at The Hideout here in a little bit. There's this ugly Christmas sweater party happening."

Quin makes a face. "I don't—"

Jason cuts him off. "You don't have to have an ugly sweater," he says with a laugh. "If Willow was here, she might force you to, though. Speaking of which, have you heard from her lately?"

"She mentioned a girls' trip to some cabin. Sugarbush, I think. After that she said she was going to be with her family for New Year's Eve."

Jason cocks his head slightly. "Weird, because Cora and Sam are at The Hideout right now."

Quin shrugs. "She took leave earlier this week. Said she was having a hard time dealing with something."

Jason nods. "Probably Emerson. You know they've been talking about those girls who disappeared? Our friend has been gone for a little while too, but Willow said she got a text from her saying she was going home because of some family problems. I guess she told Cora that she was starting to worry that didn't actually happen, because she hasn't been responding to any texts or answering calls, but sometimes people shut down when there's a death in the family."

He seems to shrug off the whole thing and doesn't appear to have any concerns about Emerson, which works for us.

Once again, Quin finds the opportunity to bring up his situation.

"Yeah, that's true. Just so you know, I'm leaving town soon. Remember I told you about my dad? Well, things are bad. I need to go home and help my mom and start planning a funeral. So, I likely won't be attached to my phone either."

Jason's lips part. "Oh, dude. That sucks. I'm sorry, man."

Quin waves it off. "It's fine. I'll be okay. Kas is coming with me."

I watch as Jason's expression changes from pity to confusion and then shock before finally settling into a blank-faced nod. "Oh. Ohh. So, you two..."

He looks at me and I wink at him. "You had your chance."

Jason blushes before turning to Quin. "Wow. Well, okay. You both should still come to the Christmas sweater party. A little sendoff party."

Quin looks at me and I know he wants me to get him out of it, but it's probably something we should do, even if it's only briefly.

"Yeah, we'll see you there."

"Great!"

"I'm going to hurt you," Quin groans once Jason walks off.

"Promise?"

EZRA

THIRTY-EIGHT

It's nearly ten-thirty when our last-minute farewell party takes a turn. Initially, everything was normal. We all shared a round of shots, the bar held their ugly sweater contest and crowned a winner, and we sat at our table with our drinks, talking and laughing.

It took about an hour and a half for the news to spread about me and Kas being together. There were a few new people around who we hadn't been around previously, and they didn't seem to care either way. It was new information to Cora, Sam, and BJ, however. The girls were fine with it, but BJ remained quiet.

For the last half hour, he's been watching us with silent disdain. The look on his face lets us know how he feels, but we're not trying to focus on him. We'll be out of here soon enough.

"Sorry about BJ, man," Jason says when he sits next to me. "He's always been a dick, so I'm not really surprised."

"Oh, so you see the homophobic rays beaming off of him, too?" Kas asks.

Jason snorts, but it doesn't hold much humor.

We watch as BJ reaches out and grabs Samantha's arm, yanking her down so he can something in her ear. Her face reveals her surprise and anger, and then her eyes flicker in our direction before she quietly says something back to him.

"He's talking shit," Kas says quietly, the fury in his eyes burning bright.

The two of them continue to argue quietly at the end of the long table before she snatches her arm away from him.

"I'm not staying here with these two fucking fags."

Jason whirls around and looks at us with wide eyes, but Kas and I stay focused on the argument on the end of the table.

"Then fucking leave," Samantha says before rushing off toward the bathroom.

"Yo, that's not cool, man," Jason says, standing up. "They're not even doing anything."

"Shut the fuck up, Jason," BJ replies.

I put my hand on Jason's arm. "It's okay. Go check on Sam."

He hesitates briefly before walking off. BJ gets up and sneers at us before stomping his way to the bar. Kas tracks every step, and I can almost read every twisted thought behind his gaze.

Soon, Sam and Jason appear next to the table.

"I'm so sorry, guys. I don't know what to say. I'm embarrassed and angry," Samantha says, her eyes red-rimmed from crying.

"Don't apologize," I say. "It's not your fault."

"I don't want to be around him," she says, chancing a nervous glance toward the bar. "Jason's gonna take me home."

Me and Kas both nod. "Sounds good. We'll probably leave soon, too."

"Take care, guys," I say.

"Have a safe trip," Jason offers. "Sorry one of your last times here ended like this. Feel free to reach out if you need anything."

I dip my chin. "Thanks."

We only stay long enough to finish our drinks. Once we're outside, Kas takes a breath, still struggling to keep his anger under control.

"My dad used to call me that a lot," he finally says between gritted teeth. "He'd say I was the way I am because of him, because of the things he had done."

"That's bullshit," I spit. "If I could bring him back from the dead, I would, just so I could fucking kill him all over again."

"I know it's not true. I am who I was always going to be regardless of him, but it was just the things he'd say to get under my skin."

I stay quiet, knowing there's not much else I can say to offer him any sort of relief. But I do know of something else I can do.

After nearly an hour, BJ emerges from the bar and gets into his sports car. It's such a stupid car to drive in the winter around here, especially considering there's still plenty of snow on the ground as well as patches of ice.

We follow him for nearly ten minutes before the slow leak in his tire from the small puncture wound we put in it, makes it harder for him to control. He pulls over, struggling to get close to the curb since there's a thick mound of hard-ened snow along the edge.

The street is dark and lined by trees, far from the busi-ness district and not too close to any residential areas either. There's no traffic and no streetlights, but we still have to be quick about it.

We pass him and park along the curb in front of his car. I give Kas a nod when he looks over at me, and then we step out.

Kaspian grabs the tire iron from the bed of my truck before we make our way toward BJ. He steps out of the car and starts checking his tires before looking in our direction.

"Oh hell," he mutters.

I slow my steps and allow Kas to take the lead. "You got a problem with your tire?" he asks, holding the tire iron over his shoulder as he looms over a crouched BJ.

"I don't need help from *you*." His final word drips with revulsion.

"No?" Kas asks. "It's late. There's only one place that'll tow you out of here and they don't return calls for hours."

BJ stands up, coming a few inches shy of Kaspian's six-foot one frame, and I stand to the side of them, waiting to see where this goes. "What do you know about fixing cars, anyway?"

"Plenty," Kas says with a wicked grin. "You just have to apologize to us first."

"Fuck that," BJ scoffs. "I meant what I said." He turns his back on Kas. A mistake. "I got someone who can come get me and he won't try to suck my dick either."

Kas inhales deeply, his shoulders rising as his anger grows.

I walk around and lean on the back door of BJ's car

where I'm able to look into his eyes. "I'd apologize if I were you."

"You can get the fuck off my car. You've always given me weird fucking vibes. I thought you were just some sort of freak, but now I know you have more than one problem."

My eyes lift to Kas behind him. He's furious. His brows are drawn in, creating a valley of furrows between them. His jaw is tense and his chest heaves with deep breaths.

Before BJ can reach the door handle, Kas tightens his grip on the end of the tire iron and lifts it from his shoulder. With one vicious swing, he smacks BJ in the side of the head, sending him stumbling to the side.

I feel a few droplets of blood hit my face before noticing his dazed, brown eyes as he stares back at Kaspian in disbelief.

Moving away from the car, I walk around to keep my view unobstructed. BJ reaches for the wound in his head, his fingers coming away with blood.

"You're fucking crazy."

"You're damn right I am, and don't think I'd ever let you get away with talking to him like that."

It looks like BJ is about to open his mouth to say something else, but Kas doesn't let him. He lets loose and swings over and over again.

BJ stumbles before falling to his knees. Kaspian hits him again. He doesn't focus solely on his head, choosing to spread the pain through his body—arms, shoulders, stomach, legs.

I keep my steps moving so I can continue to watch the rage in his face as he works, grunting and breathing with each swing.

When BJ is finally on his back, whimpering and crying, Kas barricades his waist with his feet before bringing the tire iron down on his head and face over and over until he stops making noise. Blood splatters across Kaspian's clothes and skin, and though it's cold outside, a sheen of sweat glistens across his forehead.

After a minute, he stands up straight and rolls his neck, holding the weapon at his side. He's fucking glorious.

"We should go," I say, eyeing him up and down.

He pierces me with his dark eyes. "Yeah."

We leave BJ in the snow, his blood creating crimson snow around him, and hop into my truck and drive off. We're currently staying in a motel, but I don't have the patience to wait until we get there. I drive for about two miles until I find a clearing between trees and park.

"Get out."

I don't wait for him to ask why, perhaps he already knows. By the time I get around to his side, he's already on his feet, the door closed behind him.

Before I can attack, he's on me, his hand sliding over my cheek until he cups the back of my head. His lips collide into mine as I run my hand through his hair, tugging on the strands.

"You're so fucking perfect," I murmur against his mouth, my hands moving to his pants to undo the button. "So depraved." I shove his jeans and underwear down. "Fucking magnificent."

He grins at me, his murderous eyes on mine as his teeth sink into his bottom lip. "I love how morbid you are."

My lips quirk up, and then I drop to my knees in the snow and take him in my mouth. Kaspian's hand lands on my head as he releases a hiss when I take him to the back of my throat. I worship his dick, lavishing it with the attention of my lips, tongue, and hands until he's cussing and gasping for breath.

"Oh my god," he breathes. "Quin. I'm so close."

I moan around his shaft, stroking him as his crown rests between my lips. It's not long before he grips my hair tightly in his fist before exploding on my tongue. I swallow his release before standing up, and he quickly grabs my face in his hands and devours my mouth.

When he pulls away, he turns and opens the door of the truck, reaching into the glove department.

"Fuck me," he says, handing me a packet of lube before turning around and bending over the seat.

I don't waste time, ripping open the single-use package and squirting the liquid on my fingers before inserting them in his ass and preparing him for my cock.

As I stretch him, I undo my pants with my free hand and free my already throbbing erection. With the remaining lube, I coat my dick and position myself at his entrance.

I push in slowly at first, giving him a few pumps at a leisurely pace, and then I can't handle it anymore. I grip his waist and drive into him deep.

"Yes!" he cries out.

My left hand travels to his hair, yanking slightly on the strands as I fuck him hard and fast. I'm fueled by pure lust and carnal desire, wanting only to fill him with my cum and mark him as mine. I ravish him with violent thrusts, grateful that he knows how to interpret my actions. He knows I don't hurt him to cause him pain. It's just the only way I know how to express myself, especially in these moments. He accepts my brutality in a way I think only he is capable of.

"I'm about to come," I pant, my back bowing as my orgasm takes over.

"Oh yes, baby. Give it to me," he moans.

I drop my forehead to his back and release deep inside

him, my hands clinging to his waist. After several seconds, I ease out of him and we get our clothes situated. He faces me, giving me his lopsided grin before leaning in and kissing me behind my ear.

I encircle his wrist with my fingers. "I guess we should probably leave town sooner rather than later."

"Not a bad idea."

After rubbing my thumb across his hand, I let go and find my way to the driver's seat so I can get us back to our motel where we'll pack up and hit the road.

KASPIAN

CHAPTER
THIRTY-NINE

Days after we left Soledad Square, Willow was found by the owner of the cabin. I'm glad we weren't in town and forced to react in a way that makes sense. Jason texted Quin to let him know that Willow had committed suicide in a cabin. Thankfully, it's easier to fake emotion via messages. He also informed us of BJ's murder in what's being called a car theft gone wrong. We sent our condolences and didn't think about either of them again.

Turns out the deaths of the man from the kink club and the one I found for Quin from another nearby town helped us out. The cops found out about their disappearances and linked them with the women from Soledad Square. They're suggesting a traveling serial killer—one who seems to have moved on. They'll continue to investigate, but I don't think it's anything we'll have to worry about. After all, they'll never find the bodies, plus Jason mentioned rumors of people blaming it on some guy that used to work at the theater there. Some guy named Jimmy apparently took off, and now suspicion is pointing in his direction.

We sold our trucks in New Jersey and bought another used truck for us to travel in together. We have a U-Haul cargo trailer of furniture and belongings from Quin's house with us as we decide where we're going to settle.

Small town or bustling city? North or south? We travel straight through the middle of the United States, enjoying the road trip while enjoying some indulgences. We are who we are, after all.

Turns out, Quin has a hefty savings account from the death of his parents, so we're in no rush to get jobs. I have some money saved as well, but not nearly as much as he does.

One day, as we travel through Kansas, I flip through my sketchbook. It was one of the few things I knew I needed to keep.

"You've never shown me what's inside," Quin says, still looking at the road.

"Do you want to know?"

He glances over briefly. "Yes."

"Pull over."

Five minutes later, we're in a parking lot of a gas station, and Quin shifts in his seat to look at me. "I remember seeing you with that book at The Perfect Blend. You showed a picture to one of the women and she looked amazed."

"Now, I feel like I have a lot to live up to."

I hand it over and he watches me as he takes it in his hands. Opening up to the first page, I chew on my bottom lip as I study his expression.

He doesn't look up right away, but instead keeps flipping through the pages, his fingers brushing over the pictures.

"They look so lifelike."

283

"I pay attention to detail."

He looks at me then, his eyes boring into me. "I can see that."

Eventually, he turns the book and shows me a page. "How? I didn't even know you saw me."

"I always saw you," I say. "Even in a room of a million, I'll always be able to find you."

The photo is one of him at the library. He didn't know I was aware of his presence, but I knew he was watching me from behind a shelf of books. I don't have to study things for long to remember how to sketch them. In the drawing, you can only see part of him—his leg peeking out from the side of the shelf as his hand grips the side. His eyes, the ones that send chills down my spine, stare back at me through the spaces between the shelves.

"These are very good."

I smile at him. "Thank you. I suppose you could say you were my muse."

Quintin's the star of many of the pages, even if it's just a picture of a pair of blood-covered hands, eyes, or a heart. Not the typical ones that children draw, but a real one. Ones that rest inside our bodies. Some are red and dripping blood, as if they've been penetrated with a thin, long knife. Others are as black as night—the way I've always suspected mine looks like. Everything in this book is something that belongs to him or reminds me of him, and while he's stopped many hearts, he's captured mine, so it's fitting to have it on these pages.

"Come here," he commands.

I unbuckle my seatbelt and slide over. "Yes?" I tease.

"Take out your cock."

My brows lift as I instantly go for my button and zipper. "You like my drawings that much?"

He doesn't say anything, but I don't expect him to. He doesn't use his words like most people, but I'm okay with action. He bends at the waist and takes me into his mouth.

When he's done, and while I'm trying to catch my breath, I say, "Definitely sketching that mouth next."

Quin crooks his finger at me, and just as I'm inching closer, he lets some of my cum drip from his mouth. The liquid clings to the short beard on his chin as he swallows down the rest.

"Clean me up."

I quickly grab his face between my hands and lick and suck every drop of my release from his skin. Once I've finished, he gives me a wink that sends warmth through my body.

As we're getting back on the road, I sigh and look over at him. "What if we just got an RV and traveled all the time? Pick up and go when we feel like it? Do filthy things to each other as we're parked in a lot or on the side of the road."

He stares ahead, contemplating. "I think we need to have a home base. We need a new residency. New names." He glances at me. "We can definitely find time to travel, though."

I grin, knowing he's right. We can't be nomads forever. "Okay. What're we thinking? Oklahoma?" He makes a face and I laugh. "What about Nevada?"

"I'm not a fan of the desert and dry heat."

"Alaska then," I say as a joke. He's quiet. Contemplative. "No, I was kidding. I don't want to live in a fucking igloo."

He chuckles. "I think that's a common misconception. Alaska has plenty to offer."

"Like what?"

"Wilderness, seclusion. It's vast. You know they say you can fit nineteen states inside of it?"

I bring out my new phone that we got somewhere back in Tennessee. "Let me look it up." After reading for a little bit, I say, "It's eighty-five percent land and the water coverage is the highest in the US." I tilt my head, thinking. "Sounds like lots of hiding places if you ask me."

He snorts. "No sign of igloos?"

"Funny," I say. "Plenty of animals. Wildlife could take care of some evidence." I keep reading. "Oh. You know it has one of the highest crime rates?"

"So we'd fit in," he says.

"An above average amount of rapes and assaults."

He looks at me. "So we bring down the number of rapists."

"Heroes, I'd say," I reply with a grin.

"So, Alaska?"

I nod. "Alaska."

JAMISON

EPILOGUE

Ezra and Kaspian died when they got to Alaska, but Jamison and Grayson were born. To me, he'll always be Kaspian, and I'll forever be Quintin in his eyes, but our new identities have been made. We've settled in a town outside Seward, but Alaska is a playground. There's plenty to do, whether it's hiking, fishing, sightseeing, or hopping on a cruise to see wildlife and glaciers. And, of course, hunting. We prefer the last one, but not to kill bears or moose; there are much more dangerous creatures. *Humans.*

"You guys got everything you need?" Kevin asks as he walks by with his massive backpack. "I know you ain't from around here. Make sure you got the bear spray."

We chuckle along with him. "I think we got it all," I call out. I look at Kaspian and snarl, "I fucking hate this guy."

He laughs. "We won't have to deal with him much longer." Kaspian finishes packing the side pockets of his bag before stretching his arms over his head.

His shirt lifts, exposing what was once the scar left behind from Willow's attempt to take his life. Now, a tattoo covers it up. I didn't like seeing a mark left by her. If he has any, they will be from me and me only. The tattoo artist did a phenomenal job using one of Kaspian's drawings of a bleeding heart to hide the remnants of that cut.

"Come on!" Kevin yells again.

We found him a few days ago in a pub nearby, getting drunk and talking about how he recently spent time with his niece and sister in a cabin along the coastal trail. It didn't take much coaxing to get him to slip into what people call *locker room talk.*

His niece is sixteen, but according to him, looks like she's in her mid-twenties. He was sure to drive that point home by vivid descriptions of her body. He tried being responsible by talking about stepping into the role of her dad, since he left three years ago, simply to teach her life lessons. But that quickly led into, *I could teach her a few more things, if you know what I mean.* He winked, bumping elbows with me, his laugh triggering a coughing fit.

"Oh we know what you mean," Kaspian had said, but Kevin didn't see the look in his eye.

Kevin mentioned bringing his niece up here again. Alone. But we won't let that happen.

"You guys haven't hiked up here before?" he asks as we fall into step behind him.

"Nope."

We have, but he doesn't need to know. In the year and half since we've been here, we've mapped out the best places to do what we do. Here, the trail is busy, but two miles in, if you veer to the right, away from the coastline, you can travel through some trees and come across a beautiful waterfall. The water pours violently over the cliff, mist spraying the entire valley.

Not many people venture that way, because it's not an

official trail. It's dangerous and it's not a place you can camp. Plus, there are plenty more scenic opportunities for people to visit. You can overlook the bay with a backdrop of mountains and glaciers, and lush, green trees for miles. There's usually sea life visible in the water, keeping people's attention.

Right at the point we need to turn, Kaspian splits off. "What's over here?"

"You don't need to go that way," Kevin answers. "It's rougher terrain."

Kaspian keeps going. "I think I hear water."

"Let's just go check it out," I tell Kevin as I follow behind Kas.

He huffs, pausing for a few seconds before tagging along.

The ground is slick with mud. Leaves and twigs cover nearly every square inch. Kaspian reaches behind him and pulls something from his bag.

"Bears might be trying to catch fish around here," Kevin states, yelling to be heard over the sound of the waterfall.

Kaspian keeps walking, moving closer and closer. We pull up alongside him, peering down at where the water meets the earth, spraying over jagged rocks before drifting down into a stream.

"I'm not worried about any bears," Kaspian says. "They're not the most dangerous things out here."

Kevin chuckles. "Say that when you have a full-grown one charging at you."

Kas turns, dropping his bag to the ground, and I step back. "It's probably how your niece feels when you come at her."

Kevin's eyes go wide, his hands nervously gripping at

290

the straps over his shoulders. "What?" His gaze flickers to mine.

"I've come to realize that men who feel they can joke about what they would do, could do, and might do, have already done it," I tell him.

"What the fuck are you guys talking about?"

"We remember your drunken spiel from the other day," Kas says. "If you haven't already violated your niece, you will. You have it planned out in your head."

Kevin looks scared but tries to keep a brave face. "You're both wrong. I'm gonna go. I don't have time for this shit."

Kaspian's eyes darken as his anger unfurls, and Kevin turns his back on him, his massive camping backpack covering him up to his head. It's a mistake to give your back to Kas, and one he'll soon realize. Kaspian grips the hunting knife in his hand, and with a swiftness Kevin wasn't expecting, Kas is at his back, his arm reaching around and plunging the blade into Kevin's gut.

A shocked gasp and a garbled groan leave his mouth as Kaspian removes the knife while simultaneously threading his fingers in Kevin's hair. He yanks his head back and brings the blade across his throat, blood spewing from the wound. He shoves him to the side, and his heavy backpack makes it easy to send him over the edge. We watch as he tumbles backward into the waterfall where the gushing water swallows him up.

"Fucking sicko," Kaspian mutters, wiping his blade in the mud by his feet.

I reach out and grab his jacket, yanking him into me. "I like *your* kind of sickness."

He grins. "How much?"

"Want me to show you?"

His chin dips slightly as his smile grows.

We don't journey back to the trail, instead continuing up past the waterfall, where the elevation gets to forty-five hundred feet. Eventually, we find what we're looking for, having already familiarized ourselves. The clifftop is flat and wide, allowing us room to drop our bags and sit. Over the tops of trees and in between even larger ones, we have a view of alpine glaciers in the mountains across the bay. Water stretches for miles, leading into the North Pacific Ocean.

Alaska is exactly what we needed. The serene beauty and peaceful areas we've found give us the opposite of what's constantly in our heads and hearts—ugly, loud, chaotic thoughts and desires.

We won't change who we are. As the saying goes, a leopard can't change its spots. But we don't want each other to change. We were drawn to each other for these exact reasons. We accept and need the other person to be exactly who they are, because we get precisely what we need from one another. Maybe nobody else understands, but we do. Together, we feel normal.

Kaspian leans back on his palms, looking out over the view. I scoot closer to him and put my lips next to his ear as my hand slips between his legs.

"Get on your hands and knees. You can enjoy the view while I fuck you."

His eyes flicker to mine, his lips curving into a smile. "I was just thinking I wanted to do the same to you."

"Later," I say. "At home."

Home.

It finally feels like I have one.

TO READERS

I want to thank you for picking my story up and giving me a chance. You are the reason I write. I hope to have brought you some sort of enjoyment with this book, whether you liked the spice, the darkness, or anything in between. I've only written one dark book before, but couldn't classify it as a romance due to the ending, so this is my first official dark romance and it was SO MUCH FUN! I love a good villain, and here we have two! So, I must know, who did you like more? Kas or Quin? Find me and let me know! Thanks for reading!

ACKNOWLEDGMENTS

First and foremost, I have to thank Robin from Wicked by Design, because I was such a pain when it came to this cover. Haha. I thought covers with people on them were hard, but this was the hardest cover I've had to figure out, but Robin always has patience with me and never fails to produce magic. Thank you!

Cady and Tori from Cruel Ink Editing + Design are new to my team with this book. Tori was such a dream to work with. She was quick, precise, and so kind and helpful. I'm beyond grateful for her sweet words and useful tips. Cady produced beautiful and perfect teasers for this book. I couldn't be happier with her work.

I have to thank the everybody from Give Me Books, Gay Book Promotions, The SmutHood and Gay Romance Reviews for their work on my cover reveal, release blitz, and ARC distribution.

A special shout-out to every person who read, reviewed, and/or shared any photos to help spread the word. I wouldn't be able to do this without you guys. Your time is appreciated so much!

To my beta readers, Katherine, Courtney, and Elizabeth, thank you! I'm happy to have had your early advice and opinions.

I also have to thank a new friend. Caroline, I'm beyond grateful you decided to make a book club here. You're the sweetest person I've met, and because of you I've made some amazing friends. Also, thanks for telling me your son's name. I'm sorry I named a sociopathic killer after him, but it's an amazing name! Haha. I'll try not to name any other crazy characters after your children.

Last but definitely not least, my husband. Though he was deployed during this whole process he was still the best person I had in my corner. He's always available to listen to me and answer my questions and offer advice. I love you so much!!

ALSO BY ISABEL LUCERO

About the Author

Isabel Lucero is a bestselling author, finding joy in giving readers books for every mood.

Born in a small town in New Mexico, Isabel was lucky enough to escape and travel the world thanks to her husband's career in the Air Force. Her and her husband have three kids and two dogs together, and currently reside in Delaware. When Isabel isn't on mommy duty or writing her next book, she can be found reading, or in the nearest Target buying things she doesn't need. Isabel loves connecting with her readers and fans of books in general. Keep in touch!

Sign up for my newsletter.
Join my reading group.

Milton Keynes UK
Ingram Content Group UK Ltd.
UKHW040737180324
439696UK00004B/75